HENSHAW SIX

HENSHAW SIX

SHORT STORY COMPETITION WINNERS 2023–2025

EDITED BY REBECCA COLLINS

FOREWORD BY
CHRIS CURRAN

This edition published in Great Britain in 2025

www.henshawpress.co.uk

Hobeck Books Limited, 24 Brookside Business Park, Stone, Staffordshire ST15 0RZ

www.hobeck.net

ISBN 978-1-915-817-90-7 (ebook)

ISBN 978-1-915-817-91-4 (pbk)

Cover design by Hobeck Books

To all the writers in the world, big and small, tall and short, fact and fiction

AND

To all the readers who read their words

CONTENTS

FOREWORD

As a lover of short stories (both reading and writing them) I was thrilled to be asked to produce an introduction for this anthology. It's always exciting to discover new voices and novel ways of looking at the world and this collection has those in abundance. In the following pages you'll find a truly varied array of goodies, with stories to suit every mood and every taste, along with some that may tickle taste buds you didn't even know you had.

There is something very special about short fiction. After all, our reading lives invariably begin with short stories: picture books, fables, and fairy tales, often read and reread over and over. The most powerful traditional tales have been reimagined in many different forms throughout the ages and this isn't surprising because folk tales, myths and legends so often deal with the most profound of subjects in wonderfully accessible ways. In *Cinderella*, *Red Riding Hood*, *Snow White*, and the like, we find birth, death, loss, betrayal, jealousy and reconciliation, joy and despair – all the major elements of human life

– and that's true even when the adventures involve talking animals!

Indeed, one of the many things I love about the short story form is that elements some readers might consider *childish* can still find a place in such stories written for grown-ups: stories that tackle the most significant of subjects. There's no doubt too that short fiction for adult readers numbers some of the greatest stories ever written within its ranks.

One of the joys of an anthology like this one, with no particular theme and a number of different authors, is the simple fact that there really will be something for everyone. Whether you read in the order chosen by the editor, as I did, or begin with stories that capture your interest by way of their title, their first few lines, or maybe because you spot a familiar name amongst the writers, I can guarantee you a great reading experience.

The stories in the following pages that appealed most to me may not be your favourites, but I think I can safely say that all readers will find something to enjoy in each and every one of these tales. Not only have I been thoroughly entertained by the collection, but I have also come away with new insights and much to think about.

Although each one was a quick, initial, read, I found myself having to pause, sometimes for a considerable time, before moving on to the next as I allowed myself to absorb the full impact. Often I was compelled to read a story again, sometimes several times. This could have been because my expectations had been so thoroughly overturned that I needed to see how those expectations had been set up and to ensure that the author hadn't *cheated*. (In all cases I'm glad to report that they have played scrupulously fair.) More often I returned to a story simply for the pleasure it gave me. Whether that pleasure was my delight in the construction of the piece, the beauty or aptness of the language, the wit, the intensity, or that indefinable something that's impossible to pin down.

Indeed, as I write this introduction and consider the stories afresh I'm excited by the thought of revisiting the whole collection at my leisure, as well as sharing my recommendations with friends who I know will appreciate them.

As in all the best short stories, these writers have discovered many varied and interesting ways, to shine a revelatory light on aspects of the lives we all live, whether it's through the choice of topic, the use of language or an unusual format or setting.

Love is here, of course, in explorations of finding it, losing it, unrequited love, mother love and more. Apparently mundane scenes of daily life, in domestic or work situations, reveal something surprising or even profound. Checkout queues, in a supermarket or pharmacy, provide starting points for poignant insights into love and loss. A school playing field and a doctor's surgery become scenes of comical mayhem, or excruciating embarrassment. Another doctor is tormented by doubts in a hospital delivery room. A walk near a favourite beach and the memory of a special day long ago reveal the beauty and pain of long lives and long-established loves. A funeral brings back memories of another loss altogether. The voices of children ring out as they try to navigate adult worlds.

Here too are moments of transformation that shine a fresh, often surprising, light on all that has gone before. A change of tone that unsettles the reader, but in the end serves to illuminate the subject. A few of the writers manage to switch with ease from day-to-day reality to a fantastical world and back again. Creatures from myth: werewolves, a mermaid, collide with seemingly ordinary lives, revealing heartrending truths that are all too recognisable.

Such limited word counts mean that beginnings and endings gain greater importance than those of a novel. Beginnings need to intrigue or provoke, to tempt us into the writer's world, which may be one that we wouldn't normally gravitate towards in a longer work. Once we're hooked each story manages to lead, or mislead, us towards a resolution that, even if totally unexpected, feels completely right – indeed inevitable.

Although none of the authors goes for an obvious twist in the tail ending there are unexpected reversals aplenty, where our assumptions are upended in ways that change our understanding of all that has gone before. The endings are universally satisfying, but as in all the best short fiction these resolutions may send you, like me, back to the beginning. To read once more with renewed insight, into the skill of the writer, of course, but above all into the meaning of the story.

William Trevor described short stories as 'the art of the glimpse', saying that their strength lies, not in what's put in, but in what's left out. In the following pages you'll find so much revealed in so few words. In each case the brevity of the story adding to its effectiveness.

That is the magic of the short story form and, like me, I'm sure you'll find magic aplenty in the following pages.

Happy reading!

CHRIS CURRAN

EDITOR'S PREFACE

Two-and-a-half years ago, during our third year of trading as Hobeck Books, on one bright early spring morning, one of our authors emailed us to tell us about this small but much-loved short story competition that was in danger of folding. The organisers and some of the judges, she explained, were due to retire, and they'd thus far been unable to find any successors. She had once been a prize winner in this competition and was then (and still is) a volunteer and critique writer. She wondered if we'd consider taking it on. We took a moment to consider the suggestion. We had no experience running a competition. It wasn't really that closely related to what we publish, which is crime and thrillers, or where my experience lies, which is non-fiction and academic publishing. However, the idea of doing something good for a community (in this case, the writing community) appealed to me. I'd been a school governor in the past and volunteered my services painting murals on school and library walls, but at that time, when our author approached us about this competition, I wasn't doing anything beyond working and surviving. Life was very busy and I probably should have said no. But, as the saying goes, 'ask a busy person…'. So after about five minutes of consideration. I said yes.

There hasn't been a day since when I have doubted that decision, even when I'm still up at midnight replying to entries, collating stories to send to judges, adding stories to the website, arranging winnings to be sent to successful story writers or dealing with queries about the entry fee from the furthest flung corners of the world. I love the Henshaw Press Short Story competition. It adds a sparkle to my, otherwise manic, working life. I have 'met' some amazing writers and people through running it, all at different stages of their writing career. There's so much love in the writing community for the written word, for imagination, for books, for stories and, most importantly, for each other. For the second time since we took the reins, I feel such pleasure now, at the time of writing this preface (a sunny Sunday afternoon in late September), to be publishing the winning stories in this anthology. More than that, it is a privilege that I hope I never take for granted. I wish we could publish all the entries we get, as they are all winning stories in one crucial way. Just having the courage and drive to put pen to paper (or finger to keyboard) and bring a micro-world from inside your head to life is a win in itself.

If you have bought this book, thank you. If you have been gifted this book, you lucky thing. If you have borrowed it from your mum, friend, local library, neighbour or uncle's neighbour's dog's parrot's sister then write a story about it for the next competition. However this book has found itself in your hands or on your kindle, I really hope you enjoy the stories that follow.

Go on, what are you waiting for, stop reading my jabber (do people actually read these bits of a book?). Go forth and READ!

REBECCA COLLINS
HOBECK BOOKS

NOTES ON CONTRIBUTORS

HOLLY BRANDON

Holly is the world's okay-est wife, a terrible housekeeper, and the stay-at-home mom of four adorably feral children. She was born and raised in the deep south of the United States and enjoys silence, chocolate, and mind-numbing television. She has what some might call an unhealthy addiction to writing competitions, placing first in Writer's Playground, third in the Henshaw Press Short Story Competition, and third in Flash 500's Short Story Competition. Holly also has stories published with Flash Frog, Fairfield Scribes, Elegant Literature, and the 2025 National Flash Fiction Day Anthology.

ALEX CLISSOLD-JONES

Alex lives in Oxfordshire, UK, with his cat and wife. He has had jokes and sketches broadcast on BBC Radio 4 and 4extra and was shortlisted for the inaugural David Nobbs Memorial

Trust comedy writing competition. In 2024, a musical for youth theatre was performed at the Edinburgh Fringe. Other short stories have been published online by the Aurora Prize and Southport Writers' Circle.

CHRIS CURREN

Chris Curran was born in London, but has lived for many years on the south coast of England. She has been a teacher, an actor and an editor. Working with two well-known literary consultancies she has helped guide many aspiring writers towards publication. As a novelist she has published six psychological suspense novels with Harper Collins, writing as Chris Curran and also as Abbie Frost. She regularly gives talks and lectures on all aspects of crime fiction. Chris loves short fiction and has acted as a judge for a number of awards. Her own stories have been short listed for the Fish, the Yeovil and the Margery Allingham awards amongst others. Her latest short story appears in the most recent CWA anthology, *Midsummer Mysteries*.

CLAIRE DAVIES

Claire has won prizes for both her fiction and travel writing. She often draws inspiration from where she has lived and worked as a UK civil servant and speechwriter, including Spain, Egypt and Singapore. When she's not working on the next story, she is usually out cycling. Either that, or she's blogging about her latest adventure on ClairesBigBikeRide.weebly.com, having set herself the challenge of pedalling through as many European countries as she can, from end-to-end. An account of her first epic unaccompanied ride, 'Braver Than You Think, Cycling to Self-Discovery from Land's End to John O'Groats' publishes in 2025.

MARIE DAY

Marie grew up in a small mining town in West Yorkshire, UK, and now lives with her family near Bristol. She has spent most of her life day-dreaming, teaching and writing stories. Some of those stories have made it into print including Bath Flash Fiction, Searchlights Anthology, National Flash Fiction Day and Oxford Flash Fiction. She is a previous winner of the Eoin Colfer International Children's Short Story Award, and the Henshaw Press Short Story Award. Recently she was short-listed for the Bridport Short Story Prize. Marie runs Begin Writing workshops in the Bristol area.

K. S. DEARSLEY

K. S. Dearsley, began her professional writing career as a free-lance writer for the local press. Now a prize-winning play-wright, poet and short story writer (The Jo Cowell Award, Dark Tales, Lymm Festival, Sussex Radio Playwriting, etc.), her work has appeared in numerous publications including Dark Horizons, QWF, Diabolical Plots and Daily SF. Her short story anthology, *Artists and Liars*, and her fantasy novels are available on Amazon. *Discord's Shadow*, the third in The Exiles of Ondd series, was nominated for Best Novel in the British Science Fiction Association Awards 2021. Find out more at http://www.ksdearsley.com.

GENEVIEVE FLINTHAM

Genevieve works in marketing for a big chocolate brand (but sadly doesn't get free chocolate). When she's not writing, she enjoys the occasional attempt at Stephen King's writing routine—though balancing it with a day job proved challenging. Under the pen name Gen Velzian, she writes romantasy, with Fayte & Blood being her most popular book. Genevieve lives between Somerset and Bali with her husband, Adam, and can be found on TikTok and Instagram as @worldofvieve. She's a fan of short stories where not much happens, but the character evolution is everything.

JAIME GILL

Jaime is a queer, British-born writer happily exiled in Cambodia, where he works and volunteers for nonprofits. He reads, writes, boxes, travels, and occasionally socialises. His stories have appeared in publications including *Trampset*, *Blue Earth*, *Orca*, *New Flash Fiction Review*, *Litro*, *f(r)iction*, *The Phare*, *Exposition Review* and *Phoebe*, and won several awards including a Bridport prize, and been finalists for the Smokelong Grand Micro and Bath Short Story Awards. He's Pushcart-nominated and writing a novel and too many short stories. More at www.jaimegill.com. Or find Jaime on social media: @mrjaimegill on Instagram, @jaimegill.bsky.social on Bluesky or @jaimegill on X/Twitter.

DUNCAN GOULD

Duncan grew up in Stratford-on-Avon, UK, and studied English at Southampton University. He became an actor, working on stage and TV, and also a TV scriptwriter, writing episodes of *The Bill*, *EastEnders*, *Heartbeat*, etc. He then became a teacher in the 2000s and taught English, Latin and Classical Civilisation in various secondary schools in West London and Surrey. Lately he has pursued writing once more and his short stories, three of which have been published, have been long-listed, short-listed, runners up and also winners in various competitions. He lives in Twickenham with his wife Julie and two of his grown up children

RICHARD HOOTON

Born and brought up in Mansfield, Nottinghamshire, UK, Richard studied English Literature at the University of Wolverhampton before becoming a journalist and communications officer. He has had numerous short stories published and has won prizes or been listed in various competitions. His debut novel, *The Margaret Code*, was published by Sphere, an imprint of Little, Brown Book Group, in April 2025. The voice-led whodunnit is about an elderly woman whose failing memory holds the key to a murder investigation. Richard lives in Greater Manchester. X, Bluesky, Facebook, Instagram: @RJHooton.

MICHAEL KAUKEANO SONRAY-KELLY

Michael lives in Portland, Oregon, USA, and is of Native Hawaiian descent. He is an avid traveler, a self-proclaimed outdoorsman, and a perpetual novice surfer. Currently, he spends his days adventuring with his wife and three-year-old son. He has been published in *21st Century Ghost Stories* and *Black Hare Press*. He writes often for his own enjoyment.

DAVID LONGSTAFF

Growing up in three National Children's Homes, David witnessed the varied lives of others. As a news cameraman documenting the last thirty-five years of UK and world events, he continued to experience the good and the bad of human nature. Three years ago, his wife enrolled him on a local adult education course, which inspired David to start writing. 'The Boy and The Mermaid' was his first story to gain success and, since then, he has won or been a finalist in; The Bath Short Story Award, Fish Memoir Award, Wild Atlantic Flash Fiction Awards, The Parracoombe Prize, The Bournemouth Writing Festival, and of course, Henshaw Press.

SARAH LOXTON

Sarah lives in Sussex with her husband and two unruly Jack Russells, Didi and Leo, where a perfect weekend consists of a long walk and a country pub. With a background in marketing across multiple industries, including equestrian sport, wine and music, she is now a freelance copywriter by day and an aspiring fiction writer by day and night. Having a diverse background and clients has its benefits; she finds that she is invaluable to her friends when navigating the world of squeaky bonk jazz to the more eminently listenable, or when they're faced with a bewildering restaurant wine list. Sarah had a short story, 'Baring all, published in *Words and Brushes*, a collection of international short stories inspired by art in 2020.

JAY MCKENZIE

Jay's work appears in *adda*, *Maudlin House*, *The Hooghly Review*, *Fahmidan Journal*, *Fictive Dream* and others. She has won, placed or shortlisted in Exeter Story Prize, Henshaw Short Story, Quiet Man Dave, Edinburgh Short Story, Oxford Flash Fiction Prize, Exeter Novel Prize, Alpine Fellowship, Bath Short Story Award, Bath Flash Fiction Award, Aesthetica, Bridport Prize and Commonwealth, and was recently awarded first prize in the 2025 Fish Short Story Prize. Her novel, *Mim and Wiggy's Grand Adventure* (Serenade, 2023), is followed by *How to Lose the Lottery* (Harper Fiction, 2026).

GLYN MATTHEWS

Glyn is an escaped teacher of Expressive Arts and ex-professional artist with a passion for shorter written forms. He has won or been placed in a variety of prose and poetry competitions. He often writes through the eyes of a child; innocent yet knowing, alone yet without loneliness. As an only child, he is aware that such children are more likely to become detached observers of the world without necessarily becoming participants. It is this detachment that imbues many of his created worlds, whatever the age of their inhabitants. He once asked his mother how it felt to be an octogenarian. 'I'm eighteen inside,' she replied. Glyn now writes for the child in all of us.

DENARII PETERS

Prize-winning author Denarii was born in the north-west of England but is now lost in the Lincolnshire Wolds. A former primary school teacher, she spends her days writing stories and drinking a lot of coffee. In the last three years, she has achieved longlist or better in more than seventy competitions and over twenty of her pieces have been published in various anthologies. A collection of her work, *Will You Walk into My Parlour*, was published by Crystal Clear Books in October 2024 and her debut novel, *The Reluctant Reaper*, the first of a trilogy, published in 2025. Denarii's website is here: https://denari ipeters.substack.com/.

CHRISSY PELUOLA

Chrissy writes stories because there are some things she can't explain. One day, perhaps, she will publish her novel, but until then, it will have to wait for the spare evenings.

COLIN ROTE

Colin is an ex-actor who's most memorable performance was to provide the voice for an Aardman Animations character, Rex The Runt, a purple plasticine dog. He co-founded a leadership and management consultancy that used drama in its training programmes, using many scripts written by him. He wrote this short story as a break from writing the first draft of a novel, which is now nearing completion. Colin lives in Warwickshire, UK, with his wife, and when he isn't writing, he is the musical director of a choir, drummer in a band and enjoys sketching and painting.

JAMES SCHANNEP

James Schannep escaped the United States Air Force Academy (USAFA) with a degree in English Literature and General Engineering. He is the author of the *Click Your Poison* interactive gamebook series and his first novel, *Social Vampire*, was shortlisted for the 2023 Bath Novel Award, shortlisted for The Letter Review Manuscript Prize and received Honorable Mention in the 11th Annual Writer's Digest Self-Published E-book Awards.

MICHELLE SHINN

Michelle grew up in Essex, UK, before heading North for her degree in English. After being diagnosed with breast cancer in 2016, Michelle rekindled her love for writing with a personal blog charting the highs and lows of this life-changing experience. Since completing an MA in Creative Writing at Manchester Metropolitan University, Michelle has been working on her first novel, *The Recollective*, which was longlisted for the Bridport Prize. She works in marketing to fund her passion for travelling and when she's not writing, Michelle can often be found running alongside Manchester's canals or attempting to strum a tune on the guitar.

CATH STAINCLIFFE

Cath is a best-selling, award-winning novelist, radio playwright and creator of ITV's hit series *Blue Murder*. Cath has been shortlisted for the Crime Writers' Association daggers six times, winning the Short Story Dagger in 2012. Her standalone novels tell stories of ordinary families caught up in extraordinary events, giving a voice to victims, the bereaved, survivors and witnesses. Her latest books, *The Fells and Fire on The Fells*, are mysteries set in the wilderness of the Yorkshire Dales. *The Lost Girls of St Ann's*, a family saga, is inspired by Cath's experience of being adopted and growing up in the 1960s. Cath was brought up in Bradford but has lived in Manchester since leaving university.

ANDY STEWART

Andy Stewart is a retired family doctor. He and his wife have a small vineyard in South East Cornwall, UK. He enjoys writing stories with a twist, situational humour and cosy crime. In his stethoscope-wielding days he wrote humorous articles aimed at a medical readership under the pseudonyms of Dr Basil Bile and Dr Hugh Joverdraft. Since retiring he has had short stories published under his own name in *Scribble, Write Time 2 Anthology, Gin City 2 Anthology, All Your Stories Magazine, Flash Flood Journal, Farnham Flash Festival Competition Winners Book* and the *Tothill Tales and Tittle Tattle Anthology*. He is in the process of completing a collection of short stories entitled *All The Infections That The SunSucks Up*.

JUDY WALKER

Judy Walker lives in Manchester, UK. She has been writing fiction for many years. She won the UKA Opening Pages Award in 2007 for her children's novel *Frankie*. She has won and been shortlisted in a number of short story competitions and her work has been published in anthologies and magazines (including *Mslexia*), produced on stage and broadcast on BBC Radio. Her short story pamphlet, *Crossing the Border*, was published by Red Squirrel Press in 2016.

GERRY WEBBER

Gerry lives in Edinburgh, Scotland, where he belongs to a group of local authors (The Auld Reekie Scrievers) who write for pleasure. He has published a number of short stories including works in *Far Off Places*, the *Anti-Zine*, the Iron Press (*Aliens* collection) and several Parracombe Prize anthologies. Two more stories are due for publication shortly in a collection of pieces by the Auld Reekie Scrievers (*Pulling at Threads*) which is currently in press. Much of Gerry's work is darkly humorous. Most of it, he says, is thankfully brief.

NOTE ON STYLE

We have gone for a very light touch in terms of editing these stories. Yes, you could interpret that as meaning we didn't edit them. As if! Joking aside, as they come from all over the world, we feel strongly that we want to retain the styles and voices of the authors. It is not our wish to impose consistency for consistency's sake. Some of these stories are written in American English, others in Australian, Canadian, British, Irish, New Zealand or not-my-first-language English (and how amazing is that, to be able to create art in a second language?). So please excuse variations in style of commas, quotation marks, em rules, en rules and spelling. All the variation you will see is intentional and, we hope, just one colour, or is it color, in the kaleidoscope of fiction you are about to dive into.

If you do find any errors, let us know. There is no such thing as perfect but if we can get close to perfect, we may as well try.

LOST THINGS

HOLLY BRANDON

I've always been good at finding things.

I was left on the front steps of Saint Joseph's Orphanage, a ruby bracelet gripped in one tiny fist and a handwritten note in the other. Sister Cecelia would tell the story of my arrival, grin wide and crinkled eyes twinkling. "From that day on," she'd laugh, "those little hands of yours were always clutching something."

As I grew older, I became the go-to girl for recovering what others in the orphanage had lost – dropped coins, borrowed pencils, misplaced rosaries. Lost things would whisper their whereabouts, reaching for me like a shadowed vine reaches for the sun, and I came to understand I could only find things that wanted to be found.

When I was nine, we searched the building tip-to-toe for the slipped-off ring of a visiting woman. It called to me from beneath a rusted radiator, tangled in cobwebs and unswept dust.

"I'm so grateful you found it!" the ring's owner exclaimed, returning it to her finger.

Not grateful enough, I thought, watching her leave hand-in-hand with another girl, *to take me home with you.*

"How can I be so good at finding things," I asked Sister Cecelia as she combed my damp hair that night, "when I'm just awful at *being* found?"

"Perhaps," she said, pausing to set the comb on my bedside table before meeting my eyes, "lost things call to other lost things."

I shook my head. "I'm not lost."

"Of course not, my sweet child." Sister Cecelia tucked a stray lock of hair behind my ear. "You're right here with me."

I wrapped my arms around her, inhaling comfort in her familiar scent. "I *will* find her."

She took my face in her hands, planting a peck on the top of my head. "If anyone can do it, my dear, it's you."

Sister Cecelia bid me goodnight, leaving to help the other girls prepare for bed. My pillowcase smelled of Ivory soap as it soaked up stray tears and I reached inside, retrieving my two prized possessions. I admired the bracelet's oval cut rubies, letting its delicate gold chain pool against the well-read letter I smoothed across my lap, its curling penmanship as familiar as my own.

I named her Ruby, for she is precious, but I have enough jewels. I can not keep this one. I will not return for her.

She was the only thing I never found. The day I arrived at the orphanage, a milkman witnessed a woman depositing a small bundle on the doorstep. He recalled nothing about her, other than her lavish mink coat and golden hair. She left no name, no address – no hints as to the person I might be.

When I was sixteen and the orphanage grew too crowded, I was nudged from the nest with barely stretched wings and more questions than belongings. I didn't return, but I kept in touch with Sister Cecelia through letters – until I learned I'd lost her too.

Now, for the first time in eight years, I step back into the building I once called home, the crumbling brick shell empty and cold without its beating heart. I join the line of those paying respects to Sister Cecelia, tears stinging at the first sight of her peaceful face.

"Thank you for loving me," I whisper when I reach her, clutching the wooden casket with shaking hands. "You're the only one who did."

There's a shuffle of feet behind me – a group of orphan girls in the same joyless, drab uniforms I once donned. One of the older girls, thin and pale-haired, locks eyes with mine, and something within me jolts. It's as though I'm being pulled to her by some strong, invisible force.

The feeling is not unlike the whispering caress of a lost object's beckoning, but more urgent and fierce; it's unlike anything I've felt before. The girl stares back with parted lips and shock-struck eyes, and I know she feels something too.

I step away from the casket to allow other mourners their turn, my mind a carousel. *Could this girl somehow be related to me? Did my mother have another child? Or perhaps the girl is in need of my help in some other way.*

Whatever the reason, I can't deny the pull I feel towards her, and I'm determined to learn why.

After the funeral service, I visit Mother Superior's office. She is happy to accept my offer of temporary work, and even happier to do it for room and board. "The war took so much," she says sadly, handing me a key. "The only thing it gave us more of is orphans."

The washroom's familiar scent of mildew and laundry soap hasn't changed in my absence. As a girl, I spent countless hours sorting, mending, and folding; I could match any pair of socks, their missing mates often stuck to skirts or hiding beneath tables.

I'm folding a stain-speckled blouse, still warm from the afternoon sun, when I feel that same peculiar pulling sensation from before. The pale girl walks in with a few other girls, no doubt attending to their evening chores. She pauses, glancing towards me before her eyes dart away. After a moment's hesitation, she offers me a timid smile.

"Hi." I clear my throat. "I'm Ruby. I grew up here."

"*You're* Ruby?" Her eyes grow round. "Sister Cecelia told me about you."

"She did?"

She nods, grabbing a basket of clean laundry. "She always said I reminded her of you."

Goosebumps prickle my arms. *Did Sister Cecelia notice some familial resemblance?*

She sniffs. "She was my favorite nun. The only one who…" She trails off, wiping the corner of her eye.

"She was my favorite too." I blink away resurfacing tears. "What's your name?"

"Marjorie."

The dinner bell rings. "Will I see you tomorrow?" she asks.

"Tomorrow."

———

When I enter the washroom the next day, I'm pleased to see Marjorie already there, sewing a button onto a tweed skirt. She looks up, her face lighting with a smile. "Hi Ruby."

"Hello Marjorie." I grab a basket of loose socks, trying to maintain a casual tone. "How long have you been here?" I ask. "In the orphanage, I mean. Not the washroom."

Majorie's eyes never leave the threaded needle. "Seven years."

"How old are you?"

"Turned thirteen last month."

"Happy late birthday." I pull two navy knee socks from the basket, working up the courage to ask more.

"My parents died when I was six," she provides, to my relief. "Tuberculosis. Both of them."

"I…" I drop the socks, turning to face her. "I'm so sorry."

"I still remember them." She blinks, eyes shining. "They were wonderful."

"What did your mother look like?"

If Marjorie thinks my question is odd, she doesn't show it. "She was pretty," she said. "She had full, rosy cheeks, even when we had nothing to eat but turnips – and she had long dark hair, smooth and black as a raven's wings." She brushed a tear from her nose. "Do you remember what your parents looked like?"

The balloon of hope floating inside me sinks to the floor as I shake my head. *If she's not related to me, then why did I need to find her?*

I take a steadying breath. "Marjorie, do you—"

A cry rips through the warm, soapy air. It's coming from the hallway. Marjorie and I rush to the source, a girl around five on her hands and knees, tears striping her puffy pink face.

"What is it, Caroline?" Marjorie kneels at the girl's side, gently squeezing her shoulders.

Caroline gasps her reply between heaving sobs. "I... lost... my... other... ribbon." She pulls two braids over her shoulders, one of which features a dainty red bow at its end, and one which does not.

"It's alright, darling," I say, "it's only a hair ribbon."

Caroline's sobs grow louder as she buries her head in Marjorie's lap. Marjorie pats her back reassuringly, glancing at me with concern in her eyes. "Caroline is meeting with a couple today," she explains, "who are interested in adopting her."

My stomach lurches, a familiar desperate ache clawing at a wound I thought had healed. "Don't worry Caroline," I tell her. "I'll find your ribbon."

A nun leads Caroline away with soothing murmurs. Marjorie takes off in the opposite direction, turning back to shout, "I'll search this side of the building!"

As I walk through the halls, the ribbon beckons me; I can feel its desire to be found. I step into the chapel, where silence echoes and everything's cloaked in shadows. I lower myself to the floor, crawling down the center aisle as I follow the ribbon's lead. It guides me down the fourth row back, and I feel around on the cold stone floors, shrieking in surprise when I feel another's hand.

"Who's there?" I cry, squinting in the dark. "Marjorie?" She holds out her hand, revealing Caroline's red ribbon. "How—"

Marjorie shrugs. "I'm good at finding things."

"You're..." I shake my head, trying to make sense of it all. "I'm good at finding things too."

"I know."

She always said I reminded her of you.

I collapse onto one of the benches. "Is that why I felt this strange pull toward you?" I glance up at her. "Did you feel it too?"

Marjorie takes a seat next to me. "I felt something when I first saw you," she says softly. "You called to me, like all lost things do."

"But I'm not—"

Lost things call to other lost things.

Marjorie offers a kind, timid smile. "Whether you realized it or not, you wanted to be found."

We sit in silence for several minutes as I ponder her words. *I am the lost thing.*

Marjorie nudges my shoulder, breaking through thoughts. "We ought to get this ribbon to its rightful owner."

———

Caroline's squeals of delight are far louder than those of distress, and my ears buzz with happy ringing as she flings herself upon us. I'm filled with joy and hope watching her bounce down the hall, two neatly tied ribbons swinging behind her.

"Is it possible," Marjorie asks, watching her go, "to be both immensely happy and exceedingly sad, all at the same time?"

The lunch bell sounds, and we join the stream of bodies into the dining hall, sitting down to a lunch of navy beans and cornbread.

"I do think it's possible," I say, sprinkling pepper on the bland white beans, "to be pleased a friend has found happiness, while feeling pain for not having it yourself."

"I just want someone to care about what happens to me, to ask me about my day. Like Sister Cecelia used to do."

I nod, remembering our bedtime conversations. "I miss her too."

Marjorie slams her fork down, chipping the ceramic plate. "I don't care about lace dresses or porcelain dolls or silk gloves and hats. I'd just like to belong to someone kind."

"Me too, Marjorie," I tell her. "Me too."

———

When morning comes, I visit the pawnbroker's shop two blocks over.

"Gorgeous bracelet," the shop owner says, admiring the gold and rubies. "You sure you wanna sell it?"

I nod. "It's time to let it go."

He gives me a fair sum, and it's more than enough for the adoption fee and two tickets to California.

Marjorie is sunshine bright as we take our seats on the westbound train, looping her arm through mine.

"Why California?" she asks. "Not that it matters," she hastily adds, pink cheeks glowing. "I'd happily live in a shack, as long as that shack is ours."

The strange pulling sensation warms and softens like salt-water taffy left in one's pocket. "They say there's still gold buried deep in the mountains, for those who are willing to search for it."

Marjorie beams, leaning against me with contented ease as she lifts her face to mine. "And we are *very* good at finding things."

THESE ARE THE EVENTS THAT TOOK PLACE

ALEX CLISSOLD-JONES

SCHOOL WELLBEING MANAGER
DATE: Wednesday 14 September
TIME: 5pm
TEACHER: AECJ
LOCATION: Playing Fields
STUDENTS INVOLVED: Jago Spencer-Cronk / Cosmo
Xi / Barnaby Shang

These are the events which took place today at the rugby
match, U9 Wild Geese v Montington Hall.

AECJ's first observation was of Mr Spencer-Cronk growing
increasingly agitated on the sidelines, midway through the
first half.

During a break in the match, allowing Cosmo to look for his
missing rugby boot and for players to have Vaseline re-

applied, sport goggles cleaned and a collapsed lung attended to, AECJ was approached by Mr Spencer-Cronk.

Mr Spencer-Cronk requested to know: 1) why his son, Jago – a substitute – had not been brought on yet, 2) why another boy (Cosmo) had just kicked one of his own boots into the river and 3) if any of the U9 Wild Geese actually knew what sport they were playing.

AECJ thanked Mr Spencer-Cronk for his observations, in particular to the missing boot. He sympathised with Mr Spencer-Cronk's experience as spectator but made it clear that assembling the U9 Wild Geese outside, together on the same field and without too many of them crying, should be considered a success.

AECJ explained that Jago did not appear to have his mouthguard before kick-off. AECJ expressed regret that Jago could not, therefore, legally take part if he did not have a mouthguard.

AECJ revealed to Mr Spencer-Cronk that when asked where his mouthguard was, Jago had told AECJ that it was "on the coach". AECJ had pointed out to Jago that as it was a home match, the team had at no point that afternoon sat upon, been inside or even seen a coach or similar mode of transport.

After an exchange of words, AECJ and Mr Spencer-Cronk agreed that Jago should go back to school and look for his mouthguard there.

The match continued.

Roughly five minutes later, AECJ became aware of raised voices from the assembled parents watching. Initially believing it to be disagreement over a refereeing decision – where AECJ had disallowed a try on the grounds that Barnaby had both dropped the ball on the line and pointed excessively to his backside when celebrating in front of the Montington Hall players – it soon became apparent that Mrs Spencer-Cronk had arrived and had brought a large dog (Great Dane) with her. She and Mr Spencer-Cronk were engaged in a vociferous disagreement which was upsetting the other parents, the players and the Great Dane.

AECJ paused the game, to allow some boys to calm down and remind others to start moving.

Mrs Spencer-Cronk asked AECJ – in a raised voice – why he felt it right that Jago was in both a bottom rugby team and bottom Maths set. Mr Spencer-Cronk agreed strongly with his estranged wife and proceeded to quote a section of the Human Rights Act of 1998. AECJ thanked them both for their engage-ment with Jago's academic and sporting life but suggested that they continue this discussion at another time, gently reminding them that Parents Evening (last Sunday) would have been the ideal forum.

Mrs Spencer-Cronk then sought to confirm if Jago would be receiving extra time at the end of the current match. AECJ expressed confusion as to her comment. Mrs Spencer-Cronk reiterated her question, several decibels louder. AECJ asked

Mrs Spencer-Cronk if she seriously thought that the extra time granted for Jago in academic assessments was also to be used in his sporting endeavours. Mr Spencer-Cronk demanded to know what AECJ meant by "seriously". Mrs Spencer-Cronk noted that Mr Spencer-Cronk did not need to "wade in, as always", fortunately loud enough to cover Barnaby's comment that the only extra time Jago seemed to take advantage of was at lunch. At some point, AECJ emitted a long, audible exhalation to which Mr Spencer-Cronk and Mrs Spencer-Cronk both took exception.

Although recognising that it was not the ideal moment to raise this issue, AECJ politely reminded Mrs Spencer-Cronk of the 'No dogs' rule at school. Mr Spencer-Cronk suggested to AECJ that this was not the "ideal moment" to raise this issue but that his estranged wife should take the dog back to her car. Mrs Spencer-Cronk disagreed, explaining that the Great Dane was an 'emotional support animal' for Jago and proceeded to quote another section of the Human Rights Act of 1998.

AECJ suggested that if the Great Dane could manage to procure a mouthguard for Jago then it would, indeed, be considered a great support. Mrs Spencer-Cronk did not recognise the clear humour intended in the comment and proceeded to question AECJ's teaching qualifications and mental faculties.

During this whole exchange, AECJ had noticed that a number of boys – and the Great Dane – had run over to the pavilion (out of bounds). Just as he was about to address this issue, AECJ encountered Mr Lazell (visiting music teacher) entering the field of play. After grudgingly acknowledging the unusual circumstances that were occurring around him, Mr Lazell somewhat aggressively demanded that AECJ "release" Jago for his "f***ing" harpsichord lesson immediately, otherwise the parents would be billed.

Upon overhearing the exchange, Mr Spencer-Cronk expressed frustration that he would be forced to pay, mentioning his general dissatisfaction with the money he was generally parting with, in regard to "this bloody school". Mrs Spencer-Cronk proceeded to criticise Mr Lazell harshly on his physical appearance. AECJ managed to explain that Jago had gone back to school and that Mr Lazell would be able to locate him there and proceed with the harpsichord lesson. Once completed, he could return to play in the second half of the match.

All seemed satisfied with this plan.

At half time, AECJ requested that the parents and Great Dane refrain from consuming the orange slices, as these were intended for the players. He reminded everyone that there would be a Match Tea at the conclusion of the match.

AECJ observed that various members of the U9 Wild Geese had heightened emotions. A combination of parental pressure, Great Dane, mud and general confusion over rugby had caused upset and/or hysteria. AECJ warned the boys that they would be given a minus if they continued to sneak off to the pavilion and chose to giggle amongst themselves during the team talk. He praised Barnaby's suggestion that Jago could use an orange peel as a temporary mouthguard albeit qualified with reservations as to its legal standing.

As the second half was about to start, AECJ noticed that Jago had returned from school and was now wearing a Montington Hall rugby top. When he raised this observation, Mr Spencer-Cronk explained that he had withdrawn Jago from the school during half time and had secured him a place at Montington Hall in time for the second half. AECJ pointed out that, regardless of which team he was now representing, Jago still did not appear to have a mouthguard. When the Montington Hall coach was finally located (in the pavilion with a Montington Hall mother) he urged AECJ to allow Jago to play "for everyone's sanity".

Twelve minutes into the second half, Jago approached AECJ with two of his teeth. AECJ was unable to work out exactly what had happened, as Jago's distress was inhibiting his ability to express himself clearly. AECJ paused the game to investigate further. Mr Spencer-Cronk demanded to know how AECJ had allowed this to happen. Before AECJ could remind Mr Spencer-Cronk that Jago was now a Montington Hall student, Barnaby pondered, loudly, if the mishap could have been averted if Jago had used orange peel as a mouthguard.

In the somewhat heated melee that followed, AECJ was forced to use his lanyard as a makeshift red card, with the intention of sending Mr Spencer-Cronk safely back to the touchline. Mr Spencer-Cronk chose to ignore his "sending off" and proceeded to thrust his own impromptu red card – a Sunday Times Wine Club Loyalty Card (see pastoral note) – in AECJ's face. AECJ was aware of extensive howling emanating from Mrs Spencer-Cronk.

As AECJ sought to control the situation, Mr Lazell reappeared, to report that Jago had: 1) compared learning the harpsichord unfavourably to a "Maths lesson", 2) disappeared from said lesson when Mr Lazell's back was turned and 3) just handed him a tooth.

When the School Nurse was finally located (in the pavilion with the Montington Hall coach and the Montington Hall mother), Jago was quickly taken to the Sanitorium alongside Mr Spencer-Cronk and Mrs Spencer-Cronk, Barnaby (who had suffered a light head wound from Mrs Spencer-Cronk's umbrella), Cosmo (inconsolable that "no-one" had passed him the ball "all afternoon") and Mr Lazell ("Hepatitis B").

By this point, the Great Dane had punctured the ball so AECJ concluded the match and thanked all the players for a good game. The boys were happy to get to Match Tea.

To follow up: can someone locate a Great Dane, last seen entering the cricket nets at approx. 15.34.

(update 18.30) AECJ has just found a mouthguard in his track-suit pocket, belonging to Jago Spencer-Cronk.

To follow up: AECJ to ask witnesses to clarify Jago's comments "on the coach" (see paragraph 7).

AECJ to prepare a resignation letter.

WITH EACH MOONLIGHT VISIT

MARIE DAY

It wasn't lost on Ada how she saved the best crockery for those who wanted to visit her the least. She reached into the cupboard for the large dish with the vermillion rose print. When she set it down on the kitchen counter, she noticed that the painted stems, twisting around the porcelain edges, had gathered more thorns.

She chopped the carrots, slicing the wooden board beneath like a prisoner marking the days till their release. Things could be worse. Much worse. Her mind drifted to the Hobarts, sinking into poverty because of the livestock they'd lost. Earlier in the month, Frankie Hobart had run out with a shotgun in the dead of night to find most of his sheep gone. Bones and all. Hearing the news, Ada had dropped her shopping basket onto the counter and asked whether Frankie had shot whatever killed his livestock. The others in the store snorted as though she were ignorant. *Course not. A shotgun can't leave its mark on the devil.*

Ada was relieved that the meal she had to prepare for the visit coincided with the Hobart's downturn in fortunes. In some small way, perhaps she could compensate for their losses if she bought extra meat and vegetables from their farm shop. From now on, she would buy all her vegetables there, even though she could find them cheaper elsewhere in town.

A switch from the jazz music she'd left on in the background gave Ada a start. The red needle slid across the radio dial through a range of stations. A woman gave the weather – Elvis sang *You're the Devil in Disguise* – a new band was introduced – a crackle of static grew louder and louder. Ada snatched at the off button and reminded herself odd things tended to happen on nights when he visited.

When an outside noise broke her thoughts, Ada glanced at the clock. It was too early for him to be there. Hope devoured her, and she looked from the window to the full, round moon and the yard beneath. The wind had picked up and the broken swing squealed on its single hinge. Over by the trellis, just as before the last visit, her late husband was deadheading the roses.

'Alf,' she whispered. Desperate to ask him about the whole awful situation, she ran to the kitchen door. And like last time, he was no longer there when she stepped into the garden.

The rare glimpses of him on these nights, both lifted and splintered her heart. Sometimes, she believed he was sitting at the kitchen table while she put away the food she'd bought in town. She could hear his soft chuckle as she danced clumsily between the fridge and the cupboards, hear the deep sigh when she told him about the bloodstains found in the churchyard. A churchyard of all places.

Not able to close the door on Alf, she left it ajar. By the radio was a photo of her son as a small boy. A wide, trusting smile, with a gap at the front where his new teeth were yet to grow. He'd always been shy, would cling to her skirt rather than join the other children in the park. *It'll all change* – her sister had said. *Wait till he falls for a girl. Believe me, that old saying about a daughter for life and a son till he takes a wife. All true.* The women with older sons nodded and laughed as though she were a fool whose naivety they needed to break. While the other boys threw a ball around the park, she placed an arm around her son and held him closer than ever.

Ada glanced at the clock above the kitchen door; it was almost twelve. Not much longer. No doubt her son's wife would wait until the last possible moment to decide whether she would join them. Sometimes she accepted the invite and stayed silent for the duration, her nose held high in the air, rarely making eye contact with Ada. One time she simply looked at the food and walked off. Ada had watched her make her way over the bridge towards her family's home.

More often than not, she didn't visit. Though Ada wore the hurt like a tarnished brooch when her daughter-in-law stayed away, she also enjoyed their time alone. She'd never liked the girl. Ada had warned her boy to stay away from their kind. Her son had no time for small town gossip and even less time for superstitions. But beneath its garland-decked streets and flower beds on every corner, the small town was built on the rocky foundations of myths and superstition.

At her window, the rustle of leaves spoke in a way she only understood in the thick of night. They warned of misery and an approach.

A long howl shook the night and her nerves. She wouldn't

keep him waiting. She grabbed handfuls of meat, arranged the ox hearts over the roses and placed the hunk of raw lamb in the centre of the dish that weighed heavy in her bloody hands as she stepped towards the door. The autumn air greeted her as she made her way into the night.

On a silver horizon stood the wolf. She joined him via the white wooden garden gate and placed the bowl with the roses and thorns and ox hearts and lamb on the grass before her son. He pushed the vegetables to one side, as he always did as a boy, but devoured the meat. Ada cast her gaze to the river, away from the sharp teeth tearing through muscle. At least when he ate with her she was able, in some small way, to spare the town of more bloodshed. Meal finished, he licked bloodied lips and nestled closer against her thigh. She crouched before her son and ran a hand through matted hair, sickness twisting her stomach, so close to the stench of blood and death and lost dreams.

'Could you change? For me?' Ada asked. Then added, 'As *she* doesn't care enough to be here.'

Never criticise his love. He'll only turn on you – her sister had warned.

Legs stiff, hackles raised, the wolf bared its teeth. The gums were darker and redder than they'd ever been. Ada stumbled back in fear and regret. Over the years, she'd seen less of the young man. He regularly chose to bear no resemblance to his own kin but instead mirror *her* kind. With each moonlight visit, she felt him slip further away and a part of herself die. Somewhere, in those eyes was a ghost of the boy he once was. Before love stole him away.

'No. Stay as you are.' She raised her hands in what she hoped was an apologetic wave. 'Stay however you feel...you.

Just please stay longer.'

The wolf lowered its head and padded with her along the riverside. By the silver ripples, Ada let her voice wander far away. She told him about the roses she'd laid on his father's grave, how she'd scrubbed the wooden bench that overlooked Alf's headstone.

'Mrs Fletcher at the store asked about you the other day,' she said. But Ada could feel the weak hold on her son withering to nothingness. What did he care for any of the people in town? He'd despised them since they'd moved here for Alf's work. And though Ada understood those feelings, these people had become part of her life. They did right by her when Alf passed, baked her apple pie, invited her for coffee at The Parlour or asked how she was when buying eggs at Fletcher's store.

My son? He's doing very well, thank you. He's still travelling with his new girlfriend. Loving every minute from what I gather – Ada had said to Mrs Fletcher. And with a heavy heart, *Oh dear, that's terrible –* when the old woman told of her granddaughters' kittens torn apart by a wild dog... or worse. Much worse.

'I'm doing fine for money these days. I mended some trousers for Harry Lawton, made a blanket for the Fletcher's new grandbaby and I've almost finished the curtains Harriet McColl ordered. The folk in town pay a fair wage. So, I'm fine. You needn't worry about me.'

For a moment, as clouds wandered before the moon, the wolf looked up at her and Ada let herself believe he was still the quiet boy he had always been. The one content to be by her side and simply listen. If he came to care for these people and their small town, he and his family might spare them more bloodshed and terror. If he could see that they were decent folk who'd done all they could when his own father passed, then he might go to another town where the people weren't as kind or deserving. Not that anyone deserved that. But somewhere far away where she didn't have to be reminded all the time. When he blinked and stared ahead across the river, something twisted inside Ada. She hardly ever saw him and yet there she was wittering on and on, adding her worries and tales of mundane life as a side dish every time he came for dinner.

If only she had a more interesting topic with which to snare him. Money put food on the table, but she couldn't afford the cinema or the theatre. Her one treat was a brandy at The Candlelight Lounge, playing Bridge on a Sunday evening. It was a time to bluff with tales of her son sending postcards from Vienna, Paris, Rome. *Thank goodness he found a lovely girl in college he could share those experiences with.*

Ada religiously stuck to that one drink and one game against the backdrop of Miles Davis on the jukebox. Then she made her way back to the empty house before the others got onto the topics of slaughtered animals and glowing devil eyes in the garden and the inevitable countdown to the next full moon.

Across the river, deep within the heart of the woods arose a long howl. This one set the hairs on Ada's neck on end because she knew what it meant. He would leave. The sound of his mother's voice, her wearisome stories about the townsfolk, the tears in her eyes – unable to tether him.

Goodbyes were hurried. *Be good.* The words flew from her mouth as though he were still a child about to go on a play-date. He tolerated her clinging hug before he rushed back to his life. To his new family. Alone, Ada returned to the house. She turned on the radio and allowed music to fill the home.

Rubbing her hands under the tap, she watched the blood swirl down the sink. It would be another month at least until the next visit. She looked over to the photo of her son with his shy, gap-toothed smile and felt the cold water gnaw at her bones.

A REAL PARTY ANIMAL

KARLA DEARSLEY

How did other people do it? George fumbled in his coat pocket for the door key. He knew hundreds of people and virtually all of them were one half of a couple. They had their ups and downs, but somehow, they managed to stay together, or if not, they soon found another partner. Not so George. Women said he was funny and tried to mother him, but go to a party with him? He had as much chance of being the next man on the moon.

He opened the door and was almost bowled over by a whirlwind of chestnut fur barking ecstatically. "Okay, okay, Dusty. I'm pleased to see you, too." He disentangled himself from the red setter's enthusiastic welcoming embrace, holding its front paws as if they were dancing so he could pass it in the narrow hallway. "If only I could meet a woman who'd be as pleased to see me as you are." George walked through to the lounge avoiding the dog's tangle of legs and slumped down in a chair. If he was going to arrive at Bob's party at a reasonable time, he ought to start getting ready, but he did not have the heart for it. "Going to a party on your own's no fun, Dusty."

The dog rested its chin on his knee, gazing up at him with adoring eyes. He stroked the silky ears.

"I wish I had someone like you to go with. Loyal, trusting obedient – well, most of the time – and with stunning looks."

Someone who only wanted to be with him, who never criticised him.

"You know, Dusty, sometimes I envy you. Dogs have it easy. All they have to do is eat, sleep and go for walks. Simple – no struggle to earn a living, no problems with the opposite sex. I wouldn't mind being a dog." He pushed the hound away. Time to shower and get ready. "You wouldn't make a bad-looking woman, with that red hair and those long legs."

"You think so?" The husky voice stopped George dead in the doorway. He turned slowly.

Where the setter had been there now stood the most gorgeous woman George had ever seen. He felt his jaw drop, but he could not gather his thoughts enough to close it, he could not even frame a coherent question. How did she get there? Normally he would have danced a jig at the mere thought of having such a beauty in his lounge. Her long auburn hair framed a delicate face with large liquid brown eyes. Her figure was sleek and her legs... She could not be real. George blinked hard. She was still there.

"Who are you?" he whispered.

"I Dusty." The husky voice was hesitant. George tried to place the guttural accent.

"You – Dusty?" George found his voice had developed a squeak. He looked about. Where was the dog? Not under the armchair or behind the settee. The woman watched him search. The eager, expectant way she waited was familiar, like Dusty when it was time for her walk. George covered his face with his hands. This was it. Friends had warned him he would go mad if he lived on his own too long. The woman took an awkward step forward and licked his cheek.

"Um, I don't think that's a good idea." He felt stupid talking to an hallucination, but the lick felt wet enough to be real. It was ludicrous! Dogs did not just turn into people, especially absolute knockouts wearing red lace mini-dresses and velvet chokers.

"You wish for me." The woman answered his thought. George had often thought Dusty could read his mind. She looked expectantly at him.

"Er, sit." The woman obeyed, folding up her long legs to sit on the carpet.

———

After a cold shower George felt better. He had been working too hard, that was all. A few drinks and some lively company at Bob's party were just what he needed. George strode confidently down the stairs, but all his self-assurance vanished as he opened the lounge door and peeped round it. There she was, sitting just as he had left her; beautiful as a Greek goddess and just as likely to exist. He slumped against the wall and slid onto the floor. The woman shuffled closer and tapped at his arm. Her face wore a beseeching expression. His hand automatically reached out to stroke the silky auburn hair. She looked real, she felt real, and after all, he had often thought that Dusty was better behaved than most humans. Why shouldn't he take her to a party? At least it would prove whether he really had lost his grip on reality or not.

"Come on, then."

Dusty jumped up and rushed to the door ahead of him.

"Heel! I mean, wait – please." Should he treat her like a dog or a woman? If George did not know how to behave how could he expect her to? It was not far to Bob's house but it was far enough for George's misgivings to weight each step. What if he introduced Dusty as his girlfriend and all everyone else saw was a dog? The less attractive canine behaviour bothered him, too. When he thought of the sort of places dogs sniffed, George broke out in a sweat.

Bob opened the door and his eyebrows nearly shot to his hairline. George held his breath, then his friend's face broke into a predatory smile. His gaze followed the long-legged redhead as George ushered her inside.

"You lucky dog, George. Why'd you keep her so quiet? Scared of competition?" There was an expression of incredulous admiration on Bob's face as he greeted George.

George revelled in it. "Oh, Dusty and I have known each other for years."

Bob laughed and slapped him on the back. "Just friends, eh?"

Gradually George relaxed. Dusty behaved impeccably, becoming more and more human as the evening wore on. Her speech lost its throatiness and became more articulate, but she retained her dog-like devotion to him, never straying from his side. George felt as if he had suddenly grown six inches. He ignored a persistent itch behind his ear as he watched Bob approach.

"You don't mind if Dusty and I dance, do you?" Bob smiled and held out his hand to her.

George was suddenly furious. He smacked Bob's hand away. "Yes, I do!" The room fell quiet. George had not meant to sound so ferocious, but for the first time, he had a stunning partner and he was not about to let anyone else come sniffing around.

Bob stepped back holding up his hands in denial. George knew he ought to say something, turn the incident into a joke, but he felt more like following after him, shouting insults. Dusty belonged to him, she was his girlfriend – dog – he reminded himself with a jolt. This was getting out of hand. He scratched absently and gave way to an urge to sniff her neck. She smelled human.

Dusty patted his arm. As she began drawing George towards the door he did not resist. A good night's sleep; that was all he needed and then he would feel himself again. They had barely stepped outside before he was paralysed by an awful thought.

"It's not midnight, is it? I mean, you're not going to change back?"

"No, I'm not."

George felt weak with relief as he inhaled deeply of the still night air. Now all he needed was to get rid of that darned itch. Anyone would think he had fleas. George sat back on his haunches and gave it a really thorough scratch with his hind foot. His hind foot? George looked up at Dusty with bewildered eyes. She bent over and patted his head.

"What's happening?" His voice came out as a pathetic whine.

"It's the other half of your wish. You did say you'd like to be a dog."

"Why didn't you tell me?" he howled.

Unlike Dusty, he was no pedigree, only an ungainly mongrel with a scruffy brown coat.

Dusty leaned towards him and ruffled the springy fur on top of his head. "You never asked me," she said, but he was no longer listening.

George was under the pull of a smell far more tantalising than Dusty's perfume. He sniffed the nearest lamp-post – neutered boxer, elderly greyhound, young poodle princess... Time to try out his canine chat-up lines. He might not be a handsome dog, yet he did have a certain comic appeal. He wagged his tail and trotted off.

THE CHOICE

CLAIRE DAVIES

I could easily have missed the moment it all began. I had just slowed to a stop behind a Seat Alhambra with old Valencia plates. Beyond stretched a line of stationary traffic. 'Looks like we're not the only ones trying to get out of the city,' I said, turning to Marta. It was as I reached over to squeeze her hand that I spotted movement in her wing mirror.

We shouldn't even have been in the city that day. The forecast had been for heavy rain. Marta wanted to stay at home, but I persuaded her to drive to the beach, where it was meant to be fine. We'd only been there an hour or so. I had passed most of that time watching the young family next to us, each in their own separate world. The little boy, in blue shark motif trunks and a matching bucket hat, was intent on building a line of sandcastles, undeterred by the incoming tide. Every time the water washed a castle away, he would scoop up the lumpen remains in his pudgy hands and build another on the same spot. A few feet away, under a parasol, his mother lay on a sunbed, breastfeeding a baby, while at the water's edge, out of earshot, his father paced up and down, phone clamped to his ear, presumably making business calls.

When I wasn't watching them, I'd been enjoying the sight of Marta stretched out on her back on a towel, one hand behind her head, the other holding a book. A pink floppy hat shielded her eyes from the glare. Sweat and sunscreen glistened on the fine hairs around her belly button and her feet were crossed at the ankles, blood-red toenails peeking through a dusting of sand. Not for the first time, I was wondering what this gorgeous, funny, talented woman was doing with a boring skinny bloke from Middlesborough who couldn't tan if he stood outside naked all summer.

Glancing back at the shoreline, I noticed that the father had taken the phone away from his ear and was looking at the screen. He turned towards his wife, checked the screen once more, and started walking in her direction. I looked away as my own phone pinged.

At first, I thought it was a bad joke.

'Look at this Marta – apparently we're all going to drown!'

She lowered her book. 'What?'

Then I heard identical pings all around us. Saw others reaching for their phones. Frowning. Exchanging words with their companions and strangers. Testing the waters, so to speak.

Barely half an hour later, we were in the traffic jam. Up ahead, on the balcony of an apartment block, a stout lady was pegging out her washing. Already, a pair of ample underpants were flapping in the sea breeze. I imagined her looking down and chuckling, 'What idiots, stuck in traffic on a fine day like this.'

Perhaps, from her vantage point, she saw the trickle of

water at the same time I saw it in the wing mirror. Perhaps, like me, she didn't think anything of it. It looked like someone further up the street had emptied a bucket. But in seconds, the trickle swelled to a rivulet. Within minutes, the rivulet had grown to a torrent, spilling out from the gutter, disappearing under the car, surging across the pavement. A woman walking past screamed and leapt into a doorway, trying to save her shoes. A man pushing a buggy began to run, leaving a frothing wake as the wheels churned the water.

'Noah, look!' Marta said, her voice thready with alarm. 'What do we do?'

'I don't know!'

"WARNING – IMMINENT FLOODING" the text alert had said. "EVACUATE IMMEDIATELY."

Later, at the public enquiry, questions would be asked about whether the alert was issued early enough, whether people received sufficient prior instruction about the emergency warning system, and to what extent a mistrust of messages from unknown sources played a part in the disaster. All I know is that we were completely unprepared for what happened next.

It's a very strange feeling, when your car starts to float. Cars are solid. Heavy. They're meant to stay on the road. When your car breaks down, you need a whole gang of strong people to move it. A car is not supposed to pitch up and down like a boat. I gripped the steering wheel as though it might help me stay in control. The engine choked and died.

'Noah! We've got to get out! Noah!'

Marta grabbed my right arm with both hands and shook me so hard that the bones in my neck cracked. Letting go, she unclipped our seatbelts, reached for her door handle and shoved. Nothing happened.

'*Madre mía, no se abre*! Noah! I can't open it!'

'The water must be too high – use the window!' I stabbed at the button. 'Jesus, the electrics have gone.'

We were now flotsam on the surging flood, pitching, bucking and twisting, grinding against cars that had been in front and behind us on the street. Freed from my seatbelt, I was thrown onto Marta. Grunting, she pushed me off.

'In the back!' she shouted. 'Windows!'

Brilliant, Marta, I thought, thank God for manual handles. I threw myself through the front seats and started winding down a rear window. It stopped about two thirds of the way down. I wrenched on the handle, but it wouldn't budge. It would just have to be enough. And we would have to be quick. Coffee coloured water was slopping through the window, pouring through the door seals and swirling in the footwells.

If I pause to analyse the next critical moment, I know that nobler men, more selfless men than I, would have pushed their partner through the window first. They would have got her to safety before braving the torrent again to rescue the child in the Seat Alhambra, who was beating his pudgy fists against the window as the flood waters rose to his chest, and a hat with a blue shark motif slipped over his tear-streaked face.

But there was no nobility in me that day. I was reduced to pure animal instinct.

I squeezed through the window and crawled onto the roof, clinging to the edges like a starfish. Marta was right behind me. As she reached through the window, I grabbed her forearm, but before I could pull her out, the car pitched sideways, wrenching her from my grasp and hurling me into the raging waters.

I learned later that, by some strange twist of fate, a wave carried me over the wall of a first floor balcony and deposited me on my back like a beached whale. When I opened my eyes, a stout woman was kneeling beside me, her face flanked by flapping underpants.

At the inquest, I would explain that a Ford Fiesta is a very small car. I would say that, while I am slim, I am also tall, and that once I had climbed into the back seat, there was no room for Marta until I had got out. I would hide my head in my hands and sob, 'I had no choice. I had to leave first. I had no choice.'

But alone in our bed, in the dark hours of every endless night, I would taste the coffee coloured water in my throat. I would feel on my arm the scabbing hollows carved by Marta's nails as she slipped from my grasp. And I would know the truth.

SATURDAY MORNING

GENEVIEVE FLINTHAM

THAT WHICH COMES EASILY

We were twenty-seven and both unencumbered with the type of love for our partners that we had in the early, rose-scented days. Thirty was rapidly approaching and we laughed over the fact that we were a Taurus and a Gemini, as if it meant anything. My mother had moved to Greece to find herself and your mother was growing asparagus, so we decided we had things in common.

We started sending each other asparagus memes and funny Greek phrases as if we were winding ourselves into the other's family life. We never enquired after each other's partners, except to use such damning phrases as 'If we were single, would you ever consider…'

I gave you my phone to put songs onto the office Spotify account, and you added 'Saturday Morning' by The Eels. I started thinking about you on Saturdays, and then I noticed how you always put a new social media story up on Saturday mornings, as if you were thinking about me too.

We shared a work project, and we stole off into Meeting Room 5 – the only one without a window to the office – on more occasions than the work warranted. We pretended that we were delivering outstanding service on a project that required anything but, but we were just consumed by flirty hyperbole.

At the office Christmas party, I waited for a drink at the bar in the gaudy circus tent, trapeze artists winding their way through hoops in the sky, and you pressed your hand against the back of mine. It could have been an accident. It sent a thrill through me that was more exciting, more alive, than anything I'd ever felt.

I started to wonder whether you could make a good father – after all, we were of that age where I had to think firmly about such tropes. Thirty is a kicker on an oil-slicked horizon for a woman who wants their ovaries to remain firmly in gear. I tried to weigh up with logic, but logic falls foul of emotions and emotions pretend to be logic.

He'd make a great father, my emotions told me, dressed in the straightjacket of logic, nodding in the way of a therapist. *He has those qualities…*

My emotions ran dry there. Never mind; logic can be a wily bugger, always leaving at the moment that I require actual, factual qualities.

You were fun. Of that, I was sure. After the hand-touching incident, things dialled up a notch. You added a few more songs to my Spotify playlists, enhancing my 'Deep Work' and 'Gym' collations. Soon, I was even smiling on the treadmill, as one of your songs spasmed into my ears, driving my legs to go further, harder.

I thought about you when I made love to my boyfriend. I didn't even think of it as making love anymore; it was an animalistic requirement that led to greater productivity and better skin. Both were proven facts. My emotions spun around logic again, like Christmas lights around a tree. They switched on and dazzled, hiding the fleshy green spindles underneath.

You gave me a book – *Life Of Pi* – and I devoured it, looking for the hidden meaning. Were you the tiger? Was I? Was the novel really a misunderstood love story? Did the sea represent passion? I read it twice. Who am I kidding? I read it five times and bought an additional copy so that I could highlight and annotate without you seeing my obsession grow on the original.

My boyfriend read it, too. He thought it 'must be good', given how many times I was reading it; and even though he 'never reads', he decided that it looked too enticing to forego.

He started asking me about it, and I answered in crude, short words, wishing that his disputes, his mind, wouldn't infringe on the book's copyright.

And then you started asking me about it. We discussed it at length in Meeting Room 5 – which we'd started referring to as 'The Red Room' because of the colour of the walls, only we decided to keep the new name a secret. It gave me a thrill, knowing that we had a shared Red Room, even if the only clothes shirked were our jackets after a hot lunch break.

Our discussions became a form of foreplay; I would wait for my eyes to glitter before giving a response, as if I could say forbidden things without needing to move my lips. You swallowed everything. It inflated me, the power of knowledge, of conversation, and I added 'intelligent discussion' to my list of factual qualities. I imagined you sitting at the dining table in the evening, having 'intelligent discussion' with our intelligent offspring, saying delightful things that made us all laugh, before we sent the children to bed so that we could shag on the dining table.

Sex kept interrupting my wholesome images. It felt like an end destination which could never be explored, even though my body – my ovaries – were on an important road, bombing down a motorway at one hundred miles an hour, waiting to either crash, or be rescued. Watching your hands as we sat in the meeting room, typing away on a nondescript keyboard, one strong finger twitch after another, was enough to drive me insane.

If we were fifty, things would be different, I reasoned. There is a certain expectation put upon women of a certain age who wish to birth offspring, to engage both logic and emotions in the selection of a co-pilot.

On a Wednesday afternoon, when the project had drawn on for too long and our bosses were questioning the additional time required – meaning that we had to start moving past exciting conception to birth something concrete – you told me that I'd make a great mother.

Don't be ridiculous, I told you, batting my eyelashes as if I was offended. I'm way too young to think about that, I said.

I didn't want you thinking of me as some gorged broad ready to spill; I wanted to be seen as a cirrus cloud; thin, streaking past, twisting into new and exciting shapes.

Thus was the dichotomy; I knew that I wanted children,

and yet I didn't want you to think of me as anything less than exciting. Twenty-seven is a tricky age.

As you were leaving the meeting room, I stood up at the same time and we accidentally pressed together. My buttocks set themselves on the edge of the table; your groin pressed into my lower stomach; I felt your body heat rocket right through me. Your breath smelled like porridge, and I inhaled, automatically, my eyes in line with your lips. I ached all over.

And then you were gone, disappeared from the meeting room as if nothing had happened. I sat back down, panting, feeling my heart thudding in my neck, feeling that most dangerous excitement.

Feeling alive.

I confused my anxiety for all that is passionate and right in the world. This is how it's supposed to feel, I told myself, as I waited for my legs to fill with blood and propel me back to standing. This is how love is supposed to feel.

We didn't acknowledge the incident, but later, in the kitchen, you looked at me with eyes that were almost black. You'd changed the background on your phone; it used to be a picture of your girlfriend, but she had metamorphosised into a cactus. You tapped the screen to check the time, your dark eyes drawing themselves away from my face with a mixture of longing and confusion, as if there was thick treacle between us, and I took the phone screen as a sign.

You were showing me a sign.

And it helped that the cactus was the shape of an engorged penis.

I started listening to your songs on the way to work, filling my commute with a painful type of longing that cut through the humdrum of boring Earth. Why think about the news, or getting five fruit or veg a day, or texting my mother back – or checking what time it was in Greece before calling her – when there was something more ELECTRIC waiting ahead of me on the A road, dragging me along with promises of a glittering future?

Our project finished, but we had the company messenger app. We knew it was being monitored – everything was monitored – so we kept it light. You asked how my mother was doing in Greece, and I asked whether your mother was planning on growing any other types of vegetables. In this way, we were able to keep each other injected into the normality of our lives outside of work.

Every time Mum said something remotely interesting about Greece, I told you. In turn, you sent me pictures of your mother's vegetable garden, which I found fascinating. I would zoom in on each picture – on my phone in the toilets, obviously, not on the work monitor – and try and guess what she was like. She had patterned pink gardening gloves – was she a feminine type? Would she sew patterned pink romper suits for our fresh little buds?

You sent me a picture on a Sunday once, and I was filled with burning excitement all day. You were thinking about me at the weekend. It was a picture of asparagus and poached eggs. I took my boyfriend to the farmers market and bought as much asparagus as we could find. We had it with poached eggs in the afternoon before fornicating on the sofa, condom firm between us. He wouldn't make a great dad; he didn't even realise that the sea in Life of Pi represents the hidden depths of life.

I looked at the ceiling and thought about you.

THAT WHICH COMES HARDER

I heard it first from my manager. She said it blithely, but her eyes were fixed on my face.

So exciting that he's going to be a dad, she said.

She tilted her head to one side, as if I had become unzipped and she was examining the contents. We were in Meeting Room 3 – The Blue Room – and I stayed very still, a dried husk, a tumbleweed rolling across the great road.

Not true. Obviously, I assumed it wasn't true. I cornered you in the kitchen. You wouldn't meet my eyes.

Yeah, we're really excited, you said.

But what… what about us? I said, breaking all of the rules.

There was never any us, you said, smiling weirdly.

I unzipped and it all came out. The songs, the book, the hand touch, the way you pressed me against the table. The pictures, the messages, the way you messaged me on a Sunday.

You're imagining things, you said, your eyes as light as I'd ever seen them. I don't mean to gaslight, but it sounds like you've invented a whole little world there.

You laughed, and I zipped back up and felt my insides rearrange.

THAT WHICH COMES HARDEST

"Hey." You're with them. Your wife smiles, her face blank and empty. There's no way that she ever read your favourite book five times or listened to Saturday Morning on repeat. Your daughter ignores us.

"Hey," I say, slipping my fingers between my husbands. We walk past, the supermarket aisle seeming to stretch on forever.

ALL THESE THINGS THAT I'VE NEVER DONE

JAIME GILL

Today, I'll do two things I've never done before: welcome a man into my home, and serve him a meal I've cooked.

It's all a terrible, terrible mistake.

Not just inviting Patrick for dinner, though my day's been dogged by a growing certainty I've got things wrong and tonight will end in awkwardness or humiliation. Mostly that, yes, but also the meal itself.

I can't cook and don't much care about food. For me, it's a necessary inconvenience. Since leaving my family home in Northumberland and moving across the country to Manchester, I've subsisted almost entirely on toast, jam, and tinned sausages. What *possessed* me to invite this stranger for dinner?

Oscar Wilde's ghost, perhaps.

———

It all started when I discovered "The Picture of Dorian Gray" nestled among a small pile of library books I was stamping out. I glanced up to see who'd chosen this illicit treasure, expecting some subversive literature student, and was startled by the man's height and handsome, oddly lupine face. Too old to be studying, by a few years, I guessed. He noticed my expression and turned his face towards mine with a smile which made me drop my gaze instantly.

"I hope you enjoy your read," I said as I handed him his book, something I always do, though this time I instantly worried it might be misinterpreted.

"Oh, I've read it before. But I always find Wilde worth spending more time with. Don't you?"

I nodded a sort of businesslike agreement, but didn't meet his eyes.

A week later, he set down Woolf's "Orlando" on my desk, that intoxicatingly strange tale of a man becoming a woman. I stamped it and again looked up. This time he was staring right at me, smile so wide and warm I wanted to live in it.

"Is this one any good?"

"I – I don't know. I've never read it." My blush betrayed the lie, but I was terrified this was some trick or trap. He was too ordinary to be a homosexual, surely. Not that I'd ever met one, myself excepted. He opened his mouth to say something but I pretended to remember an urgent task that required my attention in the book stacks behind me. When I turned, he was mercifully gone, though I later worried about my rudeness. I hadn't told him to enjoy his read.

Five days later, James Baldwin's "Giovanni's Room" slid onto my desk and a tiny, localised earthquake struck beneath my chair.

"This isn't ours," I stammered. I'd read of the furore this tale of tragic homosexual love had triggered in America, but that was a different, brasher country than ours. The idea of it being published in Britain, even now in 1956, seemed shocking and improbable.

"This is my own personal copy, actually, I bought it in London. I thought you'd be interested and we could discuss it some time."

I'll never understand what happened next. His kind eyes made me feel – just for one moment – safe. "Oh. Okay. Yes. Let's. Over… dinner?" I pictured two men dining together in public and could barely breathe. "At… my place?"

"How wonderful."

I scribbled my address with fumbling fingers.

"Perhaps I should have your name, too?" he said as I handed him the scrap of paper. "Mine's Patrick. I work at Barclays. The bank, the one on Market Street."

"Yes, right, hello. I'm Alistair. I work…" I glanced at the books all around me, and laughed at my absurdity. Mrs. Peterson, one of our most regular borrowers, shot a disapproving look from the romance aisle she usually haunts. For the forbidden noise, I hoped.

Patrick held out his hand and I rose and shook it. He delivered a perfectly ordinary, perfectly firm handshake, and then nodded as if a business deal had been satisfactorily agreed. He left the library with a brisk, springy step.

My brief sense of safety walked out with him, leaving me aghast at the risk I'd taken. I remembered that lecturer at the university, the science boffin said to have done something important during the War. There were whispers about an arrest, that he'd been caught in a compromising situation *with a man.* I'd wondered if the police had entrapped him some- how, but how could you find out such a thing without declaring your own guilt? The lecturer died soon after that, two years ago. There'd been local rumours that he'd taken his own life.

In comparison to that fate, my non-existent culinary skills were a minor worry – but consumed me nonetheless. I borrowed a cookbook from the library but at home realised it must have been written before the War. All of its recom- mended dishes were full of exotically rare ingredients and required an oven I didn't possess.

I went on a miserable trip to the grocer's and the butcher's, trying to find anything reasonably fresh I could conjure a meal out of. Rationing had ended last year, a full decade after the Reich's demise, but scarcity still reigned supreme in the shops. I returned home with a depressing haul of carrots, pork chops and eggs.

———

I'm chopping when the doorbell chimes. We never heard air- raid sirens in Northumberland, but they surely couldn't have alarmed me more.

As I unlatch the door, I imagine him waiting in police uniform, accompanied by a smirking colleague. Silly, even I know that. Cooking for a man isn't a crime.

He's standing alone, wearing a freshly pressed white shirt and that smile.

I apologise for my poky flat and he says his isn't much better. I suspect this is a kind lie. A banker's salary can surely stretch to more than a one bedroom on Whalley Range.

"I'm just finishing the dinner," I say with a confidence no atom in my body feels. "Make yourself comfortable."

Leaving him in a worn armchair in my living room, I glance back and realise he's the only beautiful thing I've ever had in my home. There are beautiful worlds inside my books, certainly, but this man is real and he is here.

In the kitchen I start boiling the carrots, ease the chops into a simmering frying pan, and crack eggs to make my first ever omelette. All the time, I fret about what Patrick is doing. I hope he's looking at my bookshelves and not the dull paintings my mother insisted I bring to Manchester with me, under the misguided belief these cloying watercolours of fox hunts and fly fishing might brighten my life or – perhaps – impress women.

I beat the eggs competently enough, but the butter must be too hot and I smell burning within moments of pouring. I try flipping the omelette but it disintegrates.

My moan must be audible because Patrick calls, "Is everything okay?" Oh, these thin walls!

"Yes," I squeak, as the boiling pan froths orange, and – nightmarishly, simultaneously – the chops begin burning. I grab the pan to move it but it's scalding and my hand jerks away, knocking the cooking oil so that it splashes across the stove. Flames leap in a roar like judgement. *You're a fool*, they gloat.

And then he's here with me, throwing a tea towel over the burning pans. The fire fades and dies as he calmly dials the gas off. He pulls away the browned tea towel like a magician, revealing a tableau of disaster. The chops are charred, the eggs blackened wreckage. I reach for the spatula, hoping to somehow salvage something, but he places his hand over mine – stopping me, calming me.

Nobody's touched my hand so gently since I was a child.

"I don't mean to be presumptuous, but is it possible you've never done this before?"

I somehow laugh, a little.

"Well," he says languidly. "I wasn't in the mood for chops, anyway. Do you know what I hanker for? Bread and butter. Don't suppose you have any?"

We sit in the armchairs, chewing on our pauper's supper. We talk politely about what brought us to Manchester. He was old enough to serve in that final year of the War, but says he'd prefer not to discuss it. He found work in Barclays afterwards, in the outer London suburb where he was born, and was then offered a promotion in Manchester. "Dull work, but dull didn't seem so terrible to me after the War."

"Wasn't it difficult to leave your family behind?" Behind my question lies another: *are you married?*

"Well, we both seem to have left our families behind, carelessly enough. Or perhaps wisely. Actually, my parents and I aren't close, and they're very busy with the grandchildren my older brother is producing for them at a prodigious rate. I had nothing tying me down. I still don't."

I don't dare to look at him after he says this, though he looks at me fearlessly: I can feel his eyes on my face. The memory of his hand on mine glows but doesn't prove anything except kindness.

As we finish the bread and butter, he comments on my collection of Thomas Hardys and asks which I like the best.

"No, you first. What's yours?"

Does he look briefly embarrassed?

"Well. Terrible to confess, but I haven't read any. Should I?"

"Maybe the Mayor of Casterbridge? The others do tend to be a little… dramatic. You can borrow my copy."

I'd like to talk about "Giovanni's Room", which I read in a hot-faced tumult over the previous two evenings, but I don't know how to begin and he doesn't mention it. Perhaps he's forgotten that was why we said we would meet. Perhaps it never meant what I thought he did.

An awkward silence passes over us like rain clouds, as if we've both realised at the same time that I have nothing interesting to offer him. I understand now that I've harboured another fear about this evening all along, something almost as terrible as embarrassment or humiliation. Disappointment.

Perhaps it's for the best that we let this evening peter out into polite silence. What future could there be, anyway? We met through Oscar Wilde, after all, and his life reveals the dark, lonely place where these lesser trodden roads lead.

Patrick looks for a moment at the fox hunt painting, his expression slightly puzzled, and I bite back my urge to apologise for it, to apologise for me. He notices me fidget and smiles, brightly and unexpectedly. It's as though the clouds just surrendered to the sun. And when he speaks I hear cheerful bravado in his voice, as if he too knows fear, but – unlike me – knows how to best it.

"Alistair. Did you know you're rather handsome when you're flustered?"

I shake my head. He regards me with a strange, kind sadness.

"Do you know you're handsome at all?"

No. Nobody has ever said such a thing to me.

"What a terrible shame. We'll have to do something about that."

This can only be a dream. This world has never given me much of anything, so it's impossible it would now hand over everything I've longed for, just like that. But if this were a dream, would I still be able to smell lingering smoke from the kitchen?

He pushes his plate aside and steps toward me, hand outstretched. I rise, my fingers shaking in his.

"Can I kiss you?"

Another thing I've never done before. So many things I've never done and long ago accepted I would never do. Like they lay at the end of a tunnel that had collapsed, trapping me alone in darkness on the wrong side.

His free hand takes my chin and lifts my face so our eyes meet. The darkness is breached.

GRAVITY

JAIME GILL

We were strangers tumbling through our lives on separate trajectories when we crashed into each other in a grimy bar in Luton. It was 1976 and I was in my second year doing physics at the College of Technology. A girl had just broken up with me and I'd spent three days skipping lectures and drowning my sorrows, though I wasn't sure how sorry I really was. I was alone and he sat down opposite me and grinned, regarding me with bright, dilated eyes across empty pint glasses. He asked if I wanted another, as if asking that question of a man you didn't know was totally normal. I said no and then I said yes and he laughed.

I'd found men attractive before, but buried those thoughts deep inside my brain where all the impossible dreams were interred. The idea of a man was like those huge motorbikes that sometimes roared through the hillside town where I grew up, making my bicycle wobble in their tailwinds. Exciting but dangerous, and not for someone like me. My parents had spent my whole life indoctrinating me with a fear of disasters, both physical and social, and I was not a defiant child. I followed rules, and any rebellions were small and secret.

Yet here he was, talking in a way I'd never known anyone speak. He made me think of a radio DJ, his mouth a non-stop torrent of bright, fluid, confident words. By the end of the first hour, I knew all about David's disappearing dad and his adoring mum, his two wildcat sisters and their inappropriate boyfriends, the first men he'd fumbled with age 15 under a railway bridge, about his hopes to be an actor and the TV commercial he'd appeared in. By the end of the second hour, he'd prised my own life story out of me, such as it was, dug those impossible dreams out of my head. When he asked me to come to his place for another drink, I nodded and followed. If this was disaster it was also life, and the thumping of my heart told me that I did want to live, I really did.

For half a year we slowed each other's velocities. The memories are fragmentary but sharp, like the pieces of a smashed mirror. I remember hungry kissing in a dark pub corner with "Young Americans" squalling from the jukebox. I remember him calling me pretty, how embarrassed I was to be described in a way meant for girls, and how secretly happy. I remember silly scribbled notes, morning drinking, my stupefied love for him. He was carefree and careless. We had the latter in common.

One winter morning, I woke in David's bed, shivering without his warm body to hold onto. He was standing at his window, telling me to get up. I wondered if he'd been awake all night. He took speed at weekends and I mostly stuck to beer, so we often fell asleep at different hours.

"What's the time?" I croaked, a hangover's tiny hard fists beating on the inside of my skull.

"It's morning time, sunshine. Get up, get up! It snowed last night. We have to go out."

"We absolutely don't." I dragged the duvet over my head.

"We do. It'll all melt and turn to mush soon. Come out with me before it's ruined."

I remembered he'd grown up in southern cities, where snow never settled for long. I was a northern country boy, used to white fields that stayed that way for months.

I let him pull me out of bed and drag last night's t-shirt over my head. We stumbled outside, cold wind whipping my hangover away and making my ears throb. He lost his footing on an ice patch, snatched at my arm, and we both fell, laughing. When we reached the nearest park, his grey blue eyes reflected the sunlit snow. Two nearly perfect red circles had formed on his pale cheeks. I told him he looked like a clown, a handsome clown, and he kissed me. An old man walking his dog nearby muttered in our direction, so we laughed and kissed more. The universe sang.

Newton's law of universal gravity asserts that all matter attracts all matter, with a force varying according to mass and distance. Our attraction was so strong it didn't even occur to me it could weaken, but then the distance crept between us, inch by inch. I don't remember exactly how – by then, alcohol was blurring everything – but we fell out of each other's lives almost by accident, as if helpless against invisible forces. Time sped up and got messier as the distance grew. Time dilation, Einstein calls that. We were both late. All the time, sometimes so late we missed each other altogether. Once, I was late enough to find him playing pool with a man I didn't know, arm slung over his shoulder. I'd heard rumours of other guys. Someone smashed a glass against a wall. He told me I needed help and I knew he wasn't offering. I don't remember our last conversation or even where it took place.

Somewhere in the chaos, I got kicked out of university. I retreated to my parents' semi in the Peak District and tried to breathe again in that atmosphere of silent, sour disappointment. I'd drink smuggled beer cans in my childhood bedroom and sometimes join village pub crawls with old schoolfriends. On one binge, I lost my diary. His telephone number was inside, but I didn't try to track it down. Such concentrated effort was beyond me by then. Months later, a mutual acquaintance told me he'd moved to LA. I remembered him mentioning a cousin who lived there, though the details were smudged. I wanted to feel happy for him, but just felt left behind.

I continued falling, gravity's heavy hands on my ankles. I left my parents for a bar job in Leeds. They watched me leave with sad, relieved eyes.

Over the years there were a few women and one other man, but nothing worked so I drank so nothing worked so I drank. I found catering jobs, and even held a couple down for a while. They terminated in uncomfortable conversations in depressing rooms, just like my relationships. The same phrases cropped up, too, about what a nice guy I was underneath everything, and how many chances I'd been given.

I racked up three trips to A&E and two arrests over two decades. It says everything about the life and friends I'd chosen that this wasn't considered excessive in our small, shrinking circle. I never quite buried my dreams again, but they slowly died anyway, and life became a slow, hard swim against tides of disappointment and diminishment.

In 1999, my fall ended when I crash-landed into an AA

meeting in London. An old, reformed drinking friend took me. I was a shivering, nicotine-yellow ghost by then, but I heard words inside which eventually returned me to life.

David's fall had ended in 1985, in a Chicago hospital ward people were afraid to visit. I learnt this a year into sobriety, once I'd mastered the internet and spent days searching his name. His obituary was short, written 16 years before in a gay magazine I'd never heard of by someone I'd never met. Someone who'd loved him, I hoped. I took an HIV test but wasn't surprised when it came back negative. It was all so long ago. I might have told my parents I'd avoided that disaster, at least, but they were both dead. I barely remembered either funeral.

———

I try to stay as still as I can now, to live calmly and with care. I go to AA meetings, work in a charity shop, and spend every other weekend fishing with two sobriety friends. It's a quiet life. A nice life, one I'm grateful for. My parents might finally approve of me. I live slowly as if that might in turn slow time down, having squandered so much of it. It doesn't work, of course. The years still tumble by, pulling me with them.

My memory is ragged and full of holes, a common complaint among us drunks. It's probably a kindness, overall. "For an addict, happiness is good health and a bad memory," one of my friends said once while we were fishing.

Yet sometimes I see those snow-dazzled eyes as if they were right in front of me, as if I could reach out and touch that beautiful face again. Those few memories I held onto are still vivid, still sharp. I did live, I did.

When I let myself think of David, I wish I'd been a more substantial person when we met, possessed greater mass. If I had, maybe I could have held onto him, somehow arrested both our falls. I had dreams for us, dreams I never told him. But dreams are weightless, and gravity pays them no mind.

BIP

DUNCAN GOULD

Bip.

Sometimes Evie actually wished someone would try and steal something, just to liven up the day.

Bip.

These quiet shifts, with too many well-behaved, middle class customers… That was the problem…

Bip.

…with these damn self-service check-outs…

Bip.

Which she had to stand at the end of, ready to help…

Bip.

…when someone had a problem, or couldn't figure out how to use the machines…

Bip.

Which was often…

Bip.

Or when they tried to put a bloody out-of-date coupon

through and she had to let them anyway just to keep the peace...

Bip.

Which was often...

Bip.

But... it was kind of handy being able to drift off into your thoughts.

Depending what your thoughts were, of course. Because they weren't particularly pleasant ones for Evie today. Her boyfriend Jack had broken up with her after six short weeks, when things had seemed to be going so well. That meant Evie, just twenty-one, was standing at the end of a row of self-service supermarket check-out machines – and finding herself unable to stop deeply dwelling on why Jack had broken up with her so...

Bip.

...inexplicably.

In fact work today – a really quiet shift – was a nightmare for Evie...

Bip.

It was hours of time in her own head going over and over what she thought she could have done to stop him finishing with her...

Bip.

...if anything would have worked...

Bip

...if anything could have stopped it...

"Excuse me."

Bang. Out of her thoughts and in an instant Evie went over to the self-service checkout where the till of a slightly irate woman needed proof she was over twenty-one.

"—I've been flashing my light for ages, asking for help."

"I know the feeling…" thought Evie.

But…

"I'm so sorry," was what she said, and then, in an inspired moment: "Can I see some ID?"

The thirty-something year old customer's face melted like a calving iceberg.

"Really? Oh you are silly. I'm nearly 40."

But it still made the woman's day, of course. It worked every time – with some people at least. It was in fact Evie's adroitness with diffusing customers and situations like these that had got her so many of these shifts, on the self-service checkouts. After all, everyone else hated them. But Evie was good at them, and she didn't mind until now. Until Jack. And the break up…

Bip.

Like, what did he mean when he said that thing about her skin not long before they broke up? They were in her parents' bathroom, naked, post coital, Adam and Eve after the apple, a rare opportunity as her parents were out. Her parents' en suite had one of those tri-fold mirrors above the basin where you could look at yourself from three directions, and she had been looking at her face – largely unmade up, due to the activity which had just preceded it – when she had caught sight of Jack's face looking at her in the right hand side of the tri-fold mirror. And as Jack had looked at her early twenty-something, still slightly spot-ravaged skin, he had actually looked momentarily repulsed, she had thought. Her heart had quickened. Had he really not seen her out of makeup before? A nervous smile flickered over her face. Surely that couldn't be an issue now – after what they had just done, just repeatedly, vigorously and gloriously… done?

But he had then said something about a spot cream that worked for him.

A.

Spot.

Cream.

That.

Worked.

For.

Him.

What is it about men and advice? Is it an instinctive – irritating – compulsion? The deep seated need to give unwanted advice? Evie wondered if men would have rushed up to Jackie Kennedy after her husband's assassination with a tip about a reasonably priced undertaker? Or would they have recommended an excellent rubbish clearance company after the Hindenburg disaster? Or a good lifeboat manufacturer just as they pulled the *Titanic* survivors out onto the SS *Carpathia*?

But either way, yes, Jack had looked at her and recommended a spot cream – and she had felt things had been different after that.

"Excuse me."

Evie jumped half out of her (perfect) skin and dashed over to help another hapless customer pre-weigh his shopping bag. Whoever invented these self-service counters should be forced to do this role – watching over them – for eternity, Evie thought. One hair on the scales and everything was the wrong weight. God, she hated that inventor almost as much as she hated Jack right now.

Bip.

But could Jack really be that shallow? Surely there had to be something else? No one could be that intimate, that enraptured, that emotionally and physically conjoined one moment – and repulsed by a spot the next, could they? Ugly sexist thoughts slid round her mind like coiled snakes, suggesting that, yes, indeed, he could be that shallow, that his attraction could be as transient as an outbreak of acne.

But surely that meant it wasn't really a good relation…

"—excuse me…"

Bloody Hell! What is it about people and these self-service tills! It's like an eight-hour shift of trying to show your grandparents how to work their phones! How do these people get through a day without help!

"Can I help you, sir?"

"I hope so. It's the voucher I have."

The devil stirred deep within Evie's bones. She couldn't, could she?

"Can I take a look, ir?" she said in an icy tone.

Dark thoughts stirred. Was it because he was male? From the tribe of Jack? A fellow penis bearer?

Is that why, instead of the usual soft soap waffle, she gave him: "I'm afraid it's out of date, sir. See? It ran out last month. It's very clearly marked."

There! Take that for the sisterhood you spot-criticiser! Take that from the female fraternity for being a fellow penis wrangler! Take your crappy coupon back to Jack and stuff it in his acne infested face!

"Will there be anything else, sir?"

A little crestfallen, the be-suited and booted man, over fifty, polite, educated, returned the 10 pence coupon to his pocket – to try at another store.

Bip.

———

Still two hours of this largely quiet shift to go – and most of the self-service tills were working perfectly. There WAS time to work this out in her mind, thought Evie. And she was really getting somewhere with Jack. It WAS the bathroom incident. They had stood there naked, side by side, arm in arm, and she had never felt so close, so intimate with another human being – as they stood in her parents' en suite bathroom. Then…

"-Excuse me?"

For God's sake! Can't you see I'm working out a break-up here? Have you no emotional intelligence whatsoever? Can you not operate a simple bloody self-service till yourself..?

"Yes, madam?"

The woman looked for one moment like she might have had a coupon: rage began to surge up Evie's back, bringing the hackles up on her neck like a werewolf about to defend its territory.

But no… Instead the woman simply said: "Is it Evie?"

Reality flooded its way through Evie's thoughts and the bipping madness. This woman knew her!

But she did not know this woman. Should she try to call security?

"You are Evie, aren't you?" the woman repeated.

Crunch! The shock of a real personal connection barged into Evie's inner circle of hell and jarred her to her bones. So she responded. She had to respond, respond to the slight, middle-aged, smiling woman in front of her.

"Yes."

"I'm Jean."
Bip.
"Jack's Mum."

———

It was an interesting cup of coffee. That was for sure. As they sat together in the supermarket's little cafe, nursing two coffees, Jean, a small, kind, caring woman – still somewhat incongruously holding a basket with a few groceries in it – said she had recognised Evie from pictures on Jack's phone. Many pictures. She had heard about the abrupt end to the relationship and simply wanted to say she was sorry it hadn't worked out. That she could imagine Evie would be really upset by the way it had ended so suddenly and that Jack had been really keen on her – she had seen the pictures to prove it. Indeed, Jean was at pains to say she sympathised and knew how much it must have hurt Evie to be abruptly dropped like that.

———

Evie did everything in her power to stop it coming out, against the faint backdrop of "bips" in the background. But in the end, she couldn't keep it in any longer:

"Was it the spots?" she blurted out.

Jean's face creased with kindness.

"No, dear..."

"Are you sure? Because he looked at me..."

Evie began to explain about the bathroom mirror, the tri-fold – the bloody tri-fold... But Jean interrupted.

"He's going abroad. He's volunteering. For two years. He leaves next week."

After a pause where her whole life passed in front of her, Evie said:

"Well why didn't the dickhead tell me that?"

No she didn't. What Evie said instead was: "Really?"

And the truth apparently was that Jack hadn't been able to tell Evie the truth, because he thought he wouldn't be able to go through with it face to face. That he cared too much about her and knew he'd change his mind if he tried to tell her in person the real reason.

Silence fell and absorbed the two women, like spot cream dissolving into young skin.

"So it wasn't my spots? My appearance? And he liked me."

"He more than liked you, Evie," said Jean, warmly, "but he's going abroad for two years – and he's also young, like you. Too young to be tied down, perhaps."

"Well why didn't he just say that?"

Jean just shrugged.

"Search me."

The two women looked round at the gently swarming store, silently communing with each other in a connection that stretched back to the dawn of time; and then Evie looked over at her own little perch at the end of the self-service tills.

"I'd better get back to work," said Evie, getting to her feet, "but thanks."

"It's nothing, dear," said Jean as she got to her feet too. "But perhaps you could help me with scanning my shopping, if I need it?"

And so the two women walked side by side back to the tills, through the now bustling store, to where Evie took her place at the head of the self-service tills, but not before deeply and warmly embracing Jean, and wiping a tear away from her own eye.

"Thanks again, Jean. It means a lot."

"Don't worry about it."

And Jean walked back to one of the self-service machines and started to scan the few items in her shopping basket, watched by Evie.

Bip.

Suddenly a thought struck Evie like a thunderbolt, as she saw the half empty basket in Jean's hands.

"You didn't come here to shop, did you? You came here deliberately to see me, didn't you, Jean? To help me."

Jean nodded as she bipped.

"Yes, dear. You see I knew you worked here. He told me all about you…"

Jean continued as she scanned her items.

"…and I know how it feels when things don't make sense. From bitter experience. You were owed an explanation."

Evie smiled warmly at Jean as Jean went back to scanning her shopping…

Before Jean slowly drew out…

———

…a coupon.

Evie looked at Jean…

…Jean looked at Evie…

Evie looked at the coupon in Jean's hand…

…Jean looked up at Evie…

Evie strode purposefully over to Jean…

"I think it might be out of date," said Jean, sheepishly.

"It is out of date," said Evie. "Months ago."

Evie tapped her ID into the machine.

"But let me override the till and put that one through for you, madam…"

Bip.

SANTA IS FOR LIFE AND NOT JUST FOR CHRISTMAS

RICHARD HOOTON

Something was wrong. Will looked across at his mum but Ruth was just staring at a grey building that blended with the slate sky. His older brother, Liam, seemed oblivious, engrossed in his mobile. Ruth had picked them up from school and declared they were going food shopping. But this wasn't the supermarket with its bright colours, fun trolleys and busy car park.

Huddling inside his duffle coat, hand covering its missing toggle, Will kicked at the snow that had settled around his scuffed school shoes. He'd heard it was going to be a harsh winter. He thought about his mum's warning, not to get his hopes up: there might not be many presents this Christmas. The empty feeling returned to his stomach. He hadn't done anything wrong.

'Santa will come,' Will had said.

Liam had scowled. 'No such thing as Santa, stoopid.'

Will realised there was something about going to secondary school that had made his lean and lanky brother grow meaner.

He crouched down and tried to scoop enough flakes to make a snowball, but it was all slushy, not the sort that would stick together and create something impressive. He threw the slop anyway. It splattered against Liam's arm.

'Hey, pack it in!' Liam glared. 'Mum, he's throwing crap at me.'

'Boys, behave.' Ruth grabbed each child's hand and drew a deep breath of icy air. 'Come on.'

She marched them to the door of the grey building and let them push it open. They followed her inside.

Will lingered in the doorway, duffle coat swamping his skinny frame. Hesitantly, Ruth approached a counter. Behind it was a woman even older than Will's gran, wearing a green apron as if she was a dinner lady. Liam loitered in a corner, attention snared again by his phone. Will looked around. One flickering strip light. A concrete floor. Stark white walls. Pushed against them were metal shelves that reminded him of the Meccano his granddad had convinced him was better than Lego, all nuts and bolts holding everything together rather than sleek interlocking bricks. Much stronger this way, Gramps had said. The shelves were loaded with tins, packets and cereal boxes, but it wasn't like any shop Will had ever been in. No price stickers or special offers. Just plain and dull. It smelled earthy, like sawdust and Brussels sprouts. Still, it was warmer than outside.

Ruth was gabbing away to the old woman. She gave her what seemed to be a voucher. In return, the stranger handed over some plastic bags full of shopping, then glanced at Will.

'You can come in, sweetheart.' A genial smile lit her face. 'I don't bite.'

Will hopped, skipped and jumped to Ruth's side.

'Here, I've something for you.' The woman pulled a small bag of sweets from the apron's pouch. 'Make sure you share them with your brother.'

Will almost snatched them from her.

'What do you say?' Ruth pursed her lips, eyebrows raised.

'Ta,' said Will, ripping the packet open and placing a cola bottle on his tongue, tasting the fizzy sweetness.

'Thanks ever so much.' Redness rose in Ruth's cheeks, contrasting with her pale face. 'You're a saviour.'

'It's a pleasure, love. We're here to help.'

Will returned the woman's wave as he chewed on a sour worm.

They left the building. Outside, a man with a television camera on his shoulder was standing beside a dark van with a young woman in a thick coat.

'Excuse me.' The woman stepped across Ruth's path. 'We're doing a piece for the local news on the cost-of-living crisis. We'll be filming the Foodbank volunteers but it would be fantastic to get the views of people using it too.'

Ruth's mouth dropped open, but no words emerged. Will could see panic crawling into her eyes. What was it she always said? *Why can't I ever just say no?*

'It would be a huge help to speak to you about it.' The woman flashed a toothsome smile. Her perfume made the air smell flowery.

The cameraman sidestepped, one hand twisting the lens to zoom in.

Ruth nodded, though the colour had now drained from her cheeks.

'Fabulous. Let's get your lovely boys in, too. Everyone together.'

Will found himself ushered to his mum's left, his brother to her right. Liam's head drooped. A curtain of hair shielded his face.

The woman hovered a furry microphone below Ruth's chin. 'So, how long have you been using the Foodbank?'

'Er, this is the first time.' Ruth grimaced though Will wasn't sure why. Maybe the bags she was clutching so tightly were heavy and he should offer to hold one. He'd suggest it once the lady had finished.

'And what's your situation? What brought you here?' She uttered the word *situation* as though it was as delicate as the snow turning to slush around them.

Ruth stared down the black hole of the camera's lens. She swallowed hard. 'I *do* work. I'm a carer. I visit people with disabilities when the boys are at school. It's just, after paying for all the diesel and what with the gas and electricity going up along with everything else, it's been a bit of a struggle recently.'

The woman's bright red lips scrunched into a pout. She looked down at Liam. Liam's gaze remained fixed on the ground. She looked at Will and thrust the microphone towards him.

'And how does it affect you?'

Will looked up, petrol blue eyes wide. 'I worry about the bills.' He thought about his mum's expression whenever those brown envelopes hit the doormat. 'When I'm bigger, I'll get a job to help pay for them.'

'Oh.' The woman seemed stuck for something to say.

'I don't want him to worry about things like that,' inter-jected Ruth. 'He shouldn't have to.'

'How will Christmas be?' The woman had found her voice, though it was tentative.

'Difficult.' Ruth's face curdled.

'I'm not expecting much,' added Will. 'Not even from Santa.'

Ruth stroked his mop of mousy hair. He could feel hope evaporating like the snow on the ground.

———

Will's knife scraped his plate as he cut into his beans on toast. He shovelled a forkful into his mouth, saccharine tomato sauce coursing his chin. Ruth was sitting opposite at the dining table in the cramped kitchen, hunched over Will's school trousers, the flash of her silver needle and black thread magically stitching the cotton ripped at the knee back together. Her telling off still rang in Will's ears: he should be more careful, they couldn't afford a new pair.

Will finished the piece of toast and prepared to devour a second slice. Then he stopped, realising he hadn't seen his mum have any tea. He put his knife and fork down, then pushed the plate towards Ruth. 'I'm full,' he said. 'Don't want any more.'

Ruth tied a tight knot at the end of the thread, held the trousers up and gave a nod of approval at her handiwork. She folded them neatly and draped them over the back of a plastic chair before looking at the chipped plate where a piece of lightly-browned toast lay smothered under a layer of syrupy beans.

'You sure?'

'Yeah. You finish it.'

Will pulled his Christmas list and a pencil from his pocket. The shimmering fairy lights and colourful decorations adorning houses on the journey home had given him renewed hope. Maybe this was the year that Santa delivered that bike after all. Or a PlayStation. Or some games they could all play together.

Ruth polished off the food.

'Love,' she said. 'You know you won't be getting much.'

'I can still write a list to Santa.' Will crossed out the bike. And the PlayStation. His stomach rumbled. He wrote down chocolate in his best handwriting.

Ruth turned the TV on. Will glanced up but it was just the news. 'Boring.'

'We might be on.' Ruth put the empty plate in the sink. 'Though I hope not.'

It was just dreary people droning on about politics. Then Will saw a building he now recognised and the kind woman in the green apron explaining how she divided donations into packages that would feed a family for three days. He yelped as he saw himself, his mum and his brother.

'God, I look awful.' Ruth covered her eyes. 'The camera adds more than ten bloody pounds,' she muttered. Will didn't know what she meant. She just looked like… *Mum*. Though he was pretty sure he was taller than that. The camera panned into a close-up of Will as he spoke about bills.

'Marvellous.' Ruth stared at the paint peeling from the kitchen wall. 'School run's gonna be great tomorrow.'

———

Will finished his breakfast of chewy cornflakes with a splash of milk. He preferred the ones with the tiger on the packet but hadn't been allowed them for ages. Still, it was a Saturday, best day of the week. Liam was texting someone. Ruth was finishing her own cornflakes.

Something thudded onto the doormat. Lines striped Ruth's forehead.

'I'll get it,' said Will.

He picked up the pile of letters. The envelopes weren't brown, but an array of colours. He handed them to Ruth. She stared at the bundle as if they were alien. Ripping one open, she pulled out a card with a painting on the front of three wise men presenting the baby Jesus with gifts below a large star shining in the night sky.

'Who's it from?' asked Will.

'Someone we don't know wishing us Merry Christmas.'

Liam's head jerked up. 'Why's someone we don't know sending us stuff?'

Ruth opened a second envelope, another biblical scene. Her eyes watered. 'It says I'm blessed to have two beautiful boys, to hold them close and always remember that.'

'Uggh.' Liam pretended to puke.

The third was a letter giving advice about saving money by switching broadband provider or using less electricity or cutting down on non-essentials. From the fourth one a gift card fell out. The fifth had a crisp twenty-pound note inside.

'Oh!' Ruth put a hand over her mouth.

A rap on the door. Will rushed to answer it. The postman was in his shorts, despite snow falling around him. He held a stack of boxes. 'These are for you, too,' he said.

Will took the snow-flecked packages, thinking it must be Christmas Day.

'Hang on, there's more in the van.'

The postman piled more parcels into Will's arms, then took a photo for proof of delivery. Will felt as if he was a celebrity.

He staggered indoors and dropped them on the kitchen table. Liam joined him in tearing them open like hungry wolves.

'Careful,' said Ruth. 'Let me see who they're from.'

'Tracksuits each.'

'And new trainers.'

Ragged cardboard flew noiseless flights. Paper packaging became confetti strewn across the kitchen.

'A football.'

'Handknitted gloves.'

Shrieks. Squeals. Ruth watched with a goldfish expression.

'Selection boxes.'

'Board games.'

The brothers leant back, exhausted.

'They're from people who saw us on telly.' Ruth seemed less slumped, lighter. Will wondered if the camera had somehow removed ten pounds from her shoulders. 'They want us to have a happy Christmas.'

'Come on.' Will beckoned his brother. 'It's snowing.'

They rushed outside where festive lights twinkled.

'How'd those people know where we live?' asked Liam, on their white-blanketed lawn.

'Santa knows where everyone lives. Told you he'd get us something.'

'They're not from Santa though, are they, stoopid? Why *are* people giving us stuff anyway?'

Will thought long and hard as he scooped a handful of fresh snow, the sort that sticks together satisfyingly. 'Maybe there's a little bit of Santa in everyone,' he said.

He threw the snowball, hitting Liam smack in the face.

He waited for the retaliation. But Liam just brushed it off with a grin. The boys laughed together as they played while their mum watched over them, her smile returning.

UNIHIPILI

MICHAEL KAUKEANO SONRAY-
KELLY

Kahu waited outside the stone walls of the *heiau*, the volcanic rock still warm from the day's heat, and remained calm as the crowd splashed through the moonlit river and gathered near enough that he smelled candlenut oil. Torchlight danced on the dark belly of the forest, the bamboo and palms silhouetted in gold. The flames carried a threat for this *heiau*. Strangers marched through the silent valley with torches aflame, brandishing maces and mallets and the promise of a new god's love. Kahu had seen the bonfires at other temples and knew the crowd came to burn and tear down the old ways, stone by stone, so Kahu had secreted into a polished wooden box the bones and hair of a deified ancestor, to keep the *'unihipili*, their spirit, safe and intact.

Hawai'i would be a *haole* nation. The queen now worshipped at a new altar, beneath an ironwood cross, and had abolished the ancient law of *kapu* that had bound their people to their pantheon of *'akua*. Sacred places had been deemed relics from an ignorant past, the islands too small for a people who now knew of lands which dwarfed their home and their customs. Kahu, who interpreted the will of gods now dead or dying, would diminish, destined to fade into a life of unimportance, to pull wet stems from the mud with the *mahi'ai* and eat the sour *poi* of peasants.

He sensed the encroaching crowd of converts gnashing their teeth and growling in the dark, keen to reduce Kahu's prestige, his *mana*.

A dozen torchbearers entered the clearing in a somber line, many with their faces and eyes averted. Though they claimed to worship the god named Christ, their hearts understood that this was a house of *Kū-kā'ili-moku*, the snatcher of land, the god of war. They knew it was Kū who ensured the last king's conquest of this island and had enabled these people to be born. Kū, who slept beneath ferns in the shadowed forests, would see them enter these stone walls, where none of this lout had ever been allowed. They still feared Kū, powerful and plotting, who might never permit another god to tread into his house and rip down his wooden statues. The men walked in silence and stopped before Kahu.

Those who braved to look into his eyes stood defiant, clad in imported wool and cotton. The young men sported hair and beards in the foreign style, unshaven on the sides of their heads, hair waxed and parted, growing thick from their chins and jawlines. Already they resembled the *haoles*, but Kahu knew that he too would soon abandon the simple barkcloth *pareo* wrapped around his waist, and clothe himself in coarse, tight suits to appease people he had not yet met.

Kahu recognized some in the group, those who had come

to this very place or others like it, to ask for successful feats, for strong children, for fast waves and nimble limbs.

"*Aloha ahiahi kākou*," the man at the head of the procession greeted. His was a face Kahu had never seen. Pale as the clouds, hair grey and beard red, the man stood short, fat, and barrel chested among the tall, dark-skinned locals. "*Maika'i 'oe?*" Are you well, he asked.

"*Maika'i no au*" I am well, said Kahu. He glanced at the crowd behind the stranger. They seemed to have slunk back against the edge of the clearing, beyond the row of broad leafed *ki*.

Sweat dripped from the stranger's face and pooled beneath his arms in the fabric of his long linen shirt. It was incredible that these people would layer so much over their bodies when the night air sweltered and stifled. The stranger pulled a small piece of cloth from within his vest pocket, and dabbed the drops from his forehead. "I'm sure you were expecting us," he said in the island's language.

"If you had come a month earlier I might have been defiant, but I have made preparations." Kahu said in English.

The stranger replaced his kerchief and chuckled. "I am glad you know English, because I can't speak your tongue worth a damn." He looked back at the gathered men and lowered his voice. "You know, a lot of you *Kahuna* have said one thing and done another. Buried heathen artifacts. Continued to make offerings to your *'akua*. Hell, some of you even encourage the kids to skip church on Sundays if the waves are big."

Kahu did not answer but rubbed his naked chest and looked the stranger in the eyes.

"I should introduce myself," the stranger said. "Earl

Macdonald." He held out his hand for Kahu, who did not care for the custom.

Kahu moved to embrace the man and pointed at his nose.

"We can do away with that," Macdonald laughed. "Don't need to press noses together when we can shake hands. My kin have been shaking hands for centuries." He grasped Kahu's limp fingers and shook.

In the darkness a voice shouted. "*Hui!* Macdonald! Are we to begin soon?"

Macdonald held up his hand. "Not quite yet, Timothy," he said.

"That man's name is *Kealaikekai*," Kahu said, recognizing the voice. "Why did you call him Timothy?"

"At his baptism, he took a Christian name. They all did."

Kahu frowned. Many people took new names, or multiple names, but always they took Hawaiian names, with Hawaiian meaning.

"What does Timothy mean?"

"Hell if I know," Macdonald said. "He was in the Bible. The good book." Kahu stared, uncomprehending. "Timothy took the name of an early preacher, a disciple of Paul the Apostle."

"I do not know Paul the Apostle," Kahu said.

"Well, you will, if you follow Christ. Paul is one of the more venerated figures of our faith. Man wrote half the New Testament... What does *Kealaikekai* mean?"

"The path to the sea. For he is a skilled surfer."

Macdonald only waved to the gathered, and they moved in closer, their light illuminating every face for Kahu's judgement. Half understood truths fell upon the valley. Kahu had been angry about the new god, but he recognized he knew little of the newcomers and their faith. If these young men were to garner *mana*, prestige, amongst these Christians, they'd need to learn their ways, as would Kahu. As they say: "One can think of life after the fish is in the canoe."

"You may dismantle the *heiau*," Kahu said. "But please, *mālama pono* the stones and the keepsakes you find here. I am not yet ready to desecrate all that i have spent a lifetime guarding."

Barefeet and boots marched past him. They first set fire to the few wooden effigies and *pili* grass buildings. Flames rose above the trees and illuminated the clearing. Smoke and heat lifted toward the stars. Grunts and thuds echoed in the night as the men pried and pushed the un-mortared stones from their settings, and the head-high walls tumbled down like waves.

Macdonald barked orders and drank from a silver flask as Kahu watched the demolition with dry eyes.

Macdonald offered Kahu a taste. "Bourbon," he said. "From back home. Came all the way here with barrels of it, for your king. Of course, we kept some for ourselves."

Kahu took a sip and winced, the alcohol stung his nose and burned his throat. He coughed, and Macdonald laughed.

"Want anymore?" Macdonald asked.

Kahu held a hand up. "No," he gasped.

"How did you come to learn English?" Macdonald asked.

"From English sailors, when I was young."

Macdonald took another drink and looked at the smokey sky. "I think it's close to midnight," he said. "Might want to send these boys home." He whistled, and the young men stopped their destruction. "You know, this clearing will make fertile farmland. You might want to think about tilling it yourself. You can make an honest life."

Kahu wrinkled his nose. "I had an honest life," he said.

Macdonald's belly sagged over his waist like a pig. Kahu knew he could outrun, outwrestle, out-swim the foreigner as easily as the young boys could. But unlike him, Macdonald had their attention and obedience, and Kahu decided that if he wanted the same, he should be as fat and commanding as the pale man beside him.

"I am no farmer," Kahu said. "I am a priest." He grabbed Macdonald by the shoulders and turned to face him, to show the fire reflected in his eyes. "If your god allows it, I will remain a priest."

Macdonald's wide cheeks erupted into a toothy grin. "I think God would like to see a *kanaka* minister very much," he said. "Very much indeed."

———

More than a decade later, seated in a dinghy on the Salish sea, a dark, heavyset man once known as Kahu gripped his bible as others rowed him to shore. Dozens of *kanakas*, Hawaiian workers, splashed into the frigid waters of the American continent, shadowed by towering pines and an overcast, grey sky.

Kahu, now John Kahuhipa Shepherd, prayed to Christ for health and good fortune, he and his flock now under the employ of a company of English traders. "Heavenly Father, protect these men as they step into a new land, and help them to turn the hearts of those they meet toward you, oh God." He believed not a word of his prayer, but he recited it with skill and passion. Most of his flock knew less English than a dog, and nodded along with the rhythm, heads bowed, hands clasped at their chests.

Traders from Vancouver to Oregon had established camps teeming with trappers and loggers, brothels and saloons. Shepherd led the men into the small port town, to the hastily constructed hovels where they were to bunk until they could afford something better. The voyage had been cold and rough, and each of them had longed for Hawai'i while swinging in their hammocks. The wintry air clogged their noses, their blood longed for the heat of the tropical sun. The north felt like the summit of *Mauna Kea*, where the goddess of snow froze the land in defiance of her rival's lava, but that was another country, and these men had little use for the myths of Shepherd's past life.

Most in the camp hated the look of the fat *kanaka* preacher. They soon knew him from reputation, as he stumbled through the saloon and brothel, cried in the streets and behind buildings. He howled about sin, to repent for selfish mistakes. Men in these parts asked less of God than they admitted, though they still showed their face at church every Sunday. Not *kanaka* church, no; Shepherd and his ilk held service in a wooden shack in their row of shanties near the pier.

Shepherd guzzled from a silver flask and often yelled at passing fishermen. "We used to fish," he liked to say. "We fished in waters bluer than the sky. But now we are here, rich men, praise Jesus."

At night, he stumbled into his creaking, unpainted cabin and pulled curtains over the wax-paper windows. He looked around in the dark, as if expecting Jesus himself at the pinewood table, or behind the iron stove, but he was alone.

Beneath a loose floorboard he had hidden a long box of *koa* wood. From its hiding place, he removed a garland of polished teeth strung on a braid of black hair, a bleached white arm bone, and two dried *lei* of *ki* and *lehua* blossoms. He unfurled a mat woven of *hala* leaves, and on the mat, spread an ornate piece of barkcloth, on which he set his belongings.

Wheezing in the cold, he bowed his head as he had done in secret each night since the dismantling of his *heiau*, and he spilled tears for *Kū-Ka'ili-moku*, of the snatched land, who Kahuhipa killed daily in his prayers to Jesus Christ.

THE BOY AND THE MERMAID

DAVID LONGSTAFF

His body sways as he stares down at the gurgling water swirling beneath him. Would anyone care if he was swept out to sea? He pushes off on one leg and jumps across the gully. His foot slips as he lands causing him to buckle. His knee cracks against the granite and both palms slap the greasy surface. He levers himself upright, he can't even leap over a gap in the rocks. The shame of last night is still raw and he stumbles forward. A tiny beach appears, large boulders creating sides to a deep inlet. Head down he steps from ledge to ledge clambering lower until the soles of his shoes crunch on the shiny stones. He crouches, plucks a flat black pebble between his finger and thumb, walks to the water's edge, and flings it into the grey sea. It skims twice before sinking. He turns and sees her.

She's sitting with her back against a rock, cigarette in one hand, lighter in the other.

His mouth drops open. He's never seen a mermaid before.

"You're blocking my view," she says, extending an arm in front of her and waving it from side to side.

He turns to the sea and then back to the mermaid.

"Cat got your tongue?" She lifts the cigarette to her mouth, takes a long drag, then, with her chin snapping up and down, releases perfect smoke rings that rise and drift towards him.

"Shit here, isn't it," she says, looking around at the plastic bottles and washed-up shoes lying stranded on the beach. She curls the cigarette into her palm, wraps her thumb over the tips of her fingers and flicks the butt into the air. There's a hiss as it joins others floating in a brackish rock pool.

"Don't talk much do you."

His mind is blank. He can't think of anything to say. He looks up to the rocks he clambered down.

"Mummy waiting, is she?"

"No, I've got work soon."

"Ooh, he's got a job. What do you do big man?

"Work on the pier." He straightens his back and puffs out his chest. "On the dodgems.

"No, you don't."

"What? Yes I do."

"You don't work on the dodgems."

Why did he say the dodgems, the pier was enough. "Not yet but I will soon."

"Sit next to me." Her tail swishes back and forth and she pats the ground next to her. "I won't bite you."

Feeling gangly and clumsy he tramps toward her. He can't help but stare at her tail. It's black and rubbery with white scars etched deep into the surface. It separates into two fins, there are fishing hooks and bits of line tangled around it and one fin has a big chunk missing from it. The bit where she stops being a fish and starts being a girl is hidden because her t-shirt is pulled down, but he can see the outline of her chest through the thin fabric.

"Why don't you take a picture?"

His eyes flash to her face. She has her head angled down to her shoulder, eyelids wide apart and her tongue sticking out.

He laughs kicking at the driftwood and tangled netting.

"Sit down."

He slumps to the floor. He can smell her now, it reminds him of the bins he has to empty full of snotty seafood.

"Is this where you live?" she says, curling her lip at the rubbish around them.

"What on the beach! No way. The bloke that runs the fair on the pier, he owns bedsits."

"Good for you." The lighter sparks and she slips the flame back and forth under the fingers of her other hand. "You've run away."

"No. Just…"

"Same here." She kills the lighter, lifts her tail, and slaps it down again. "I didn't run though." A smell of rotting fish fills his nostrils, and he tries not to gag.

"How long have you been here?" she asks.

"A couple of months." He looks down at his dirty trousers and scuffed shoes. "How about you?

"A couple of months."

He turns to the sea. "Why don't you go back?"

"Why don't you?"

He nods and lifts his wrist. "Better get going, can't be late."

"Nice watch."

"Someone gave it me."

"Generous."

"Not really." He stands.

"Do me a favour," she says, looking up at him, "come back with some chips later. I'm starving."

"Yeah, all right." He turns, then swings back. "It'll be dark. I won't find you."

"Meet me under the pier then."

He smiles. "Okay."

His wet shoes squelch as he trots onto the wooden boards of the pier.

"You're late." A hand grabs him by the collar yanking him backwards. It's Mr Perks, his meaty fingers swell with heavy jewellery as he twists his fist and slices the lad's neck with a gold sovereign. "Why do you think I gave you a watch?" The lad wriggles but the man pulls him closer, wet lips graze his cheek and he can smell onions and cigarettes as his boss whispers in his ear. "I can easily find another boy to work for me." He releases his grip and pushes a nicotine-stained finger hard against the lad's chest. "Late again and you're back on the street."

The lad runs to the tin shack behind the penny arcade. He turns the handle and shakes the door in its flimsy frame before banging it open. Two grey rats scuttle out of the dark and across the threshold. He steps into the gloom, grabs a sack and scoops up soft toys ready to fill the glass cabinets of the claw machines. A screw-top jar, full of chewing gum balls, sits on a shelf. The lad watches as wasps crawl lazily over the coloured orbs. As he leaves, he reaches forward grips the glass sides and shakes the contents hoping to squash the insects before throwing it in the bag. As he wedges the door shut, the lights, lining the pier on loops of black power lines, flicker into life.

Speakers crackle and buzz before music drowns out the screech of the circling gulls.

Saturday night rolls into Sunday morning, the pier grows silent, and the lights disappear into the dark sky. Workers crowd together by the exit gates. The lad watches as Mr Perks hands out brown envelopes containing the wages for the week.

"You haven't finished yet," says Mr Perks, holding the lad's packet between finger and thumb.

The lad is guided through the darkness by the boss's firm hand on his back. The sea whispers below and unseen bunting cackles in the breeze. They stop at a *No Entry* sign tied to a metal gate at the very tip of the pier. The lad is shaking and his stomach is cramping with fear. Mr Perks fumbles with the lock then pushes him through the gap and points to the floor. The lad drops to his knees, sliding in the sticky excrement from the seabirds and the slime from the sea. One weak security light throws shadows across the planked floor and the lad closes his eyes. When his ordeal is over Mr Perks pushes him away with the sole of his shoe and drops the envelope. The lad has to grab quickly before the breeze lifts it over the railings and out to sea.

The newspaper is almost cold and leaks vinegar into his hands. A red glow bounces in the air below the pier and he stumbles toward it, trying not to cry.

"You took your time." The glow brightens as she sucks in the smoke and he sees her sitting at the foot of one of the huge pillars. "The lights went out ages ago," she says. "Did you bring the chips?"

He squats next to her and unwraps the food.

The Mermaid flicks a burning ember into the dark and plunges a hand into the greasy fries throwing them into her mouth. She tilts her head back and he can see her throat moving up and down as she swallows the sticky clumps. Within moments the food has gone.

He looks at the scraps lying on the sand around her.

She burps loudly and then scrapes between her teeth with a fingernail.

"What happened then?"

"Nothing." He blinks away tears and compresses the paper into a tight ball with his hands. A seagull hops forward from the shadows followed by another. He hurls the wrapper in their direction.

"I could help you," she says, watching the fighting gulls. "We could kill two birds with one stone." She smiles at her own joke and lights another cigarette. In the flare of the flame he notices two of her fingers are missing, bits of shrivelled skin hang in their place. A fly crawls toward the edge of her eye and as she shakes her head more lift from bald patches on her head.

"I want to go home," she says.

He rolls his lips tight together and clenches his fists.

"I miss the sea." He hears her tail move sluggishly back and forth in the sand.

"Just go." He wipes his eyes and points to the waves. "Swim back."

"It's not that easy." Her eyes are fixed on the horizon. Moonlight rolls across the surface of the grey water. "I will have to say I'm sorry."

"Say it then. Just say sorry and then you can go back."

"Sorry comes at a price." She turns her head towards him. "My father is cruel, he will not back down until I pay."

"What does he want? What do you have to pay?"

"Too much." She looks back to the sea. "He wants a soul."

The lad swallows, he's not sure what she means.

Laughter cuts through the darkness as a group of people stagger onto the beach. He looks across to see if they have been spotted but no one notices them. The promenade lights are still lit, and he watches as the figures throw down blankets in the orange glow.

He lowers his voice and turns back to the mermaid. "A soul?"

"I would have to take someone back with me."

"To live in the sea with you?"

"No, they would die, so I can live." She drops her head in her hands and the flies swarm again.

He wipes his salty cheeks with his fingers. "I'll do it," he says. "I'll go with you into the sea."

The mermaid lifts her head, "You'd do that for me, why?"

"Because I love you." The lad has never said those words before and it feels good. "I love you and I will do it." He immediately crouches on one knee, and curls one arm under her tail and the other around her back. He stands, staggering with her weight. He has made his decision. Slowly step by step he walks into the water. His feet sink into the wet sand and the waves lap at his ankles. He struggles forward until the mermaid becomes weightless, her body floating in the dark sea. He keeps walking the water rising over his waist. He still has hold of the mermaid's arms. He feels a tug as she flicks her tail and slips from his grasp. She's free, going home. He hears shouting from the beach and turns to look over his shoulder. People are running towards him waving their arms. He wades further into the sea. His jaw is trembling and his back is rigid with the cold. His palms are flat on the water and his eyes strain for a glimpse of the mermaid. His breathing is shallow and fast. Where is she? Has she left him? He hears splashing, her tail slapping the water. She has come back for him. Salty droplets hit his face and hands close around him. He feels her pulling him toward her. He laughs, everything is going to be okay she won't let him die.

FLO

SARAH LOXTON

Mrs Pritchard was definitely a purple. Maybe a lavender purple, but not fresh, newly bloomed lavender, more like lavender at the end of summer.

Her daughter was harder to read. Children like Flo often were. Flo stood by her mother's side in the queue in the pharmacy. She was more a haze of indeterminate colours that bled into each other and took on a different hue each time I looked. I wondered what Mrs Pritchard saw when she looked at her daughter.

Flo glanced up at her mother cautiously and all around her. She snuck out a tiny hand to the shelf next to where they stood in the aisle. Little curious, probing fingers danced over the plastic of the labels, over the shelf and fingered each bottle and tube and box before stopping on the brightest packaging. She edged the box forward, but the movement caught Mrs Pritchard's notice and brushed the little fidgeting fingers away. Disappointed, Flo looked around again before staring at me. I smiled. She smiled. She was becoming less hazy to me now; oranges and yellows unfurled around her.

'Who's next, please?' the cashier called. The elderly man in front shuffled to the till, and the queue moved forward a step. I slid in behind Flo and ran my fingers over the cool plastic labels, the cold metal shelf and rows of products. I reached the box that had caught her attention; the label read, *Pretty-in-Pink Hair Glitter*. I wiggled it forward until it was right on the edge of the shelf, teetering. Her little mouth made a perfect O, and her eyes lit up with delight. I glanced each way, winked at her and then nudged the box over onto the floor. I clapped my hands delightedly, Flo squeaked, and Mrs Pritchard whipped round. She picked up the box and replaced it on the shelf, narrowed her gaze and held her hand out expectantly. Flo's expression dropped.

'Sorry.' I mouthed.

Flo turned away and held her mother's hand obediently. They stepped forward again. This time to the desk.

'Prescription for Pritchard, I got a text to say it was ready.'

The cashier turned to a row of white paper bags on a counter behind her, all labelled and waiting.

'Peterson, Price... Pritchard, here it is.' The cashier was easy to read, the soft pink of a dusky sky. She returned to the till with the largest bag and called over the pharmacist. The pharmacist took Mrs Pritchard to one side, and the women spoke in hushed voices, pointing at different items in the bag periodically. It didn't matter, I could still hear them. Mrs Pritchard took the bag from the pharmacist and nodded in thanks.

'Come on, we need to get back.' She ushered Flo back through the shop.

Flo followed her mum down the aisle, looking up at me as she went.

'See you tomorrow,' I whispered.

———

'There's nothing there, Florence, and we have to stop having this conversation. Look how exhausted you are, too. Come on.' Mrs Pritchard righted Flo's jacket and did up the zip as she spoke.

We'd just been playing pooh sticks on the bridge and were still breathless from running backwards and forwards across the wide bridge, trying to spot which stick would emerge first. We'd dropped the sticks over the rough stone wall, raced to the other side and waited to watch the sticks appear in their slow, dizzying spirals in the eddies of the stream before tearing back across the bridge to do it again.

'Mum, it's just a game,' Flo answered quietly.

I tried to speak up too, but Mrs Pritchard had already turned away, and Flo was following behind.

'One more game Flo, one more!' I called, but Flo didn't look back. She'd been yellow and gold today, all day, sunflower yellow.

I dropped the last stick from our pile into the current below but didn't race across to see its progress this time. I peered over the low wall, looking for my reflection in the ripples and dances of the water.

———

I sat outside on the window ledge, breathing in the sweet honeysuckle that grew up the trellis around me, waiting until Mrs Pritchard had turned off the light and left the room. But instead of going to Flo straight away, I followed Mrs Pritchard downstairs.

'How is she?' Mr Pritchard closed his laptop as we entered the living room.

I stepped forward to try and answer, to find the words, 'She's—'

Mrs Pritchard cut in, 'I'm worried, Steve, she's not eaten much at all today, and she's so tired all the time.'

Mrs Pritchard was still purple, but it was faded and fraying at the edges as fatigue settled over her, too.

Mr Pritchard was more of an olive green, a sun-bleached green with a hint of earth to it. 'Sounds like she overdid it yesterday, that's all.'

'I can't stop her being a child.' Mrs Pritchard clenched her fists in her cardigan as she sat down.

'No one said we should love.' Mr Pritchard rested his hand on her leg. 'Anyway, we can't jump to conclusions before we get the results back.'

I left them to it. I'd tried to reassure them before, but they were hard to reach. 'You get some rest; I'll sit with her.' I said as I went back up to the bedroom.

Flo was fast asleep, and I didn't want to wake her, so I curled up on the foot of her bed. She woke with a start at one point, but I reassured her that I was there, and she fell back asleep.

In the morning, we played with Flo's teddys and dolls. She sat them in rows and diagnosed what illness each one was suffering from. We checked their heart rate and temperature, bandaged some of them and prescribed their medicine, mostly M&Ms.

'Who will look after us when you go?' Flo gave voice to one of the bears.

Flo and I hadn't talked about when we'd go or what it would be like. Flo shrugged her shoulders as she adjusted his new sling. 'Not sure, Tobias, but you'll be ok. In fact, I need you to look after Mum and Dad when I go.'

I rubbed her back gently. 'I'll pop back to check on them all.'

———

Not long later, well, it didn't feel like long, maybe a few weeks, I lose track, Flo was asleep in bed, but it was daytime, and it wasn't her bed.

Pink hair glitter fanned out across her pillow where it had nothing to cling to. Mr and Mrs Pritchard dozed fitfully in rigid chairs next to the bed; their fingers unconsciously gripped the armrests, and their jaws clenched even in sleep.

Tobias was nestled under Flo's arm, and I quietly slipped in under the blanket, careful not to disturb any of the tubes or wires. I kissed her forehead gently.

She opened her eyes, 'Is it time to go?' Her voice soft.

'Yes.' She was still sunflower yellow, a hundred petals catching sunlight.

'Are you coming with me?'

'Of course.' I answered.

'Will there be M&M's?'

'Lots.'

'The yellow ones are my favourite.'

'I know.'

'Pardon darling?' Mrs Pritchard leant over the bed, eyes dewy. She brushed her fingers over Flo's cheek and adjusted the pillow. 'It's ok, we're here.' She whispered.

'I know,' smiled Flo.

I reached my hand up and cupped Mrs Pritchard's face as 100 sunlit petals began to fall.

BUT SHE'S A FLAME

JAY MCKENZIE

While I was licking Gisella's neck with a whisky-scorched tongue, down the hill, a woman was burning. She sat in a chair in front of the TV while hungry, orange flames and acrid smoke devoured her. What they're not saying (but everyone knows) is that it was the husband. Husband on paper, ex-husband in heart and bone and mind. The neighbour saw him sharking around for weeks before and is only too happy to regale stories of macabre blue and white disco lights pounding the night air in the weeks running up to New Year's Eve.

We're fugged and hornet-mad in the morning from the booze and the noise and the plummeting realisation that this year will be the same as the last or worse. Gisella wants to start by getting down there to have a look: I accuse her of grief-tourism, and we have our first fight of the year before the ink has even dried on the opening headlines.

A salt-wind musses the venom from our hair and our argument as we wind down the hill.

I just want to pay my respects, you know? she says.

Someone I recognise from the party is also paying his respects by vomiting in the gutter outside the deceased's house.

Fuckin' hell, mutters Gisella.

A fence has been erected around the charred husk of the house, and I find myself wondering whether the firies or cops brought their own barrier or had to call some poor-fuck fencing contractor from the arms of a lover or dancing on a table in the lost hours to fence off a burnt house. Police are still there, and a fire engine, though the remains of the house emit a little more than a wet smoulder into the mist. A dark whimper all that's left of a life.

It was me what called them, a middle aged woman in slippers tells an assembled group of sticky beaks. *I said, he's been here and he's going to do something bad, but would they listen?*

A nearby cop shakes his head, mouths something.

We stand side-by-side for a few minutes, inhaling the char.

Who even was she? I ask.

What? Because you don't know her, so her death isn't important? Gisella's eyes are blazing, and I wonder again where she's been storing this righteous anger for the past year.

I force myself to gaze into the fathomless reds of her eyes. *No. I mean in general, like who was she? Like what was her name and stuff? Did she like popcorn? Why was she home alone on New Year's Eve?*

————

It wasn't a New Year's Eve party where I met Gisella: it was a party designed to stave off the misery of January and the bitter disappointment that set in when the freshly minted gym memberships had already found themselves relegated behind the Zaraffas loyalty card and a receipt for paracetamol. Friend of someone's sister who said *Anna, meet Gisella. Everyone's been saying you two should meet.*

All night, I stared at her bird-bone wrists and the mechanics of her knuckles rolling cigarette after cigarette, pinching them between fingers that tapered like pale thin candles.

We're not so different, you and me, she said, and I scrunched my face all tight because of my freshly pressed shirt and my neat bob. She was Medusa curls and six-months-backpacking-round-Thailand chic. *No seriously,* she said. *We both want to see and feel and be.*

I did want to see and feel and be – *do* want to see and feel and be – but sometimes the thinking gets in the way. When we discuss things – and Gisella never tires of discussing IMPORTANT THINGS – I bring logic. Gisella argues with her heart and teeth. I crave a small mortgage on a neat house: Gisella wants to dip her toes in mountain streams.

———

She wants to go to the funeral, as I knew she would.

But we didn't know her, Gis, I say. *Why would we go to her funeral?*

Don't you get it? It's not about knowing her. It's about sisterhood, standing strong in the face of toxic masculinity.

They haven't charged him, I say.

She folds her arms over her chest, foot tapping a tattoo on the concrete. *Your internalised misogyny is showing there,* she says.

Facts, I want to yell. *How can facts be misogyny?* But I don't say it because she's been agitated since New Year and I'm sucked in the lethargy of a month dragged on too long.

The other thing I want to say but don't is that the funeral is on our first anniversary.

———

Funeral etiquette where I'm from is steeped in tradition: we drive or march en masse, a sea of obsidian, clean hats, decked in pressed jet, heads dipped, faces flat. The longer we leave our eyes to gather a bulging pool of purple beneath them, the better, but we must remain stoic and dignified. Wear your grief on your face, but not in the tremors of your body. Too dramatic is frowned upon, unless you're a child. *She did so well*, they'll say if you earn your brownie points by being just the right degree of sad. We must grieve, is the rule, bow and scrape and pander to the lord of death. But not too much that it gets embarrassing.

I want mine to be colour and light and dancing, says Gisella. *Candles, incense, rose petals scattered. Barefoot and magic.* She's made a nod to her own ideals by wearing a jade silk halterneck under her grey jacket. *See, it's all about how you look at things. Some cultures really celebrate death. We dress up like lobotomised badgers and drag ourselves through mud in iron boots.*

I have gone traditional: sensible black shoes, a black skirt, black shirt. I am death's wet dream and as itchy as though my clothes are made of horsehair. We sit at the back amongst people who knew her, and people like us.

That must be the son, says Gisella, pointing at a tall thin man with the whisper of a goatee clinging to his chin. His head is hunched forwards, curling in on the rest of him like a cooked prawn.

Poor bugger, I think. Especially if it was his dad that did it.

On the way out of the church, Gisella hugs the boy, though her patchouli embrace does nothing to lighten his deadwood stare. *Thank you for coming,* he says mechanically. Someone – perhaps an aunt – presses a hand between his shoulder blades. I touch his arm, mumble something, shuffle after Gisella.

*I just can't…*says Gisella striding on. *I mean, how do you go on? Your mother of all people…*

Some people have more complex relationships with their mothers, Gis, I say and I'm thinking of myself and the uptight, pressed lipped, resentful martyr that brought me up. *You disappoint me. As always,* she said the last time I saw her.

Gisella's mother brews spiced chai in a metal teapot and has embraced all of Gisella's lovers as though they had been sent by a higher being to cast light and radiance into their lives. *Yeah, but still,* she says. Then: *Let's get drunk,* and she has marched into a sticky looking boozer before I have the chance to respond.

Happy anniversary, I mutter, running my fingers across the box in my pocket.

———

We're lying in bed, and my fingers are still slick with Gisella. Her breath is sour and so is mine. We wear matching indelible purple kisses of cheap house red.

Problem is, she says, *that kid's fucked.*

She's slurring a bit. I'd hoped the fumbling, late-afternoon sex would bring her mind back from the boy and the burning woman and back to us and our first anniversary, but she's stuck there.

Gis, I interrupt, *happy anniversary.*

I'm slurring too but it doesn't matter because the gentle blurring of the edges takes away the sting of Gisella ignoring my bid for a celebration of us. In the pub, she kept talking about how the woman must have felt, what the neighbour saw, the crushing inevitability of a woman slain by her deadbeat ex. Halfway down the second bottle, she wept on the table, and I shushed her, twining her pinging curls between my fingers. I was done with it then, and I'm done with it now.

What? she says, frowning.

Anniversary, I repeat. *One year of you and I. Our union. Our love.*

I think she snorts, but it could have been a cough. She's got that half-look that could signal either sleep or a party, so I lean off the edge of the bed and hope it's the latter.

I love you, I say. *Marry me.*

In my idle musings about this moment, I didn't picture us drunk and too hot. I didn't hear my voice as flat as a city puddle, nor Gisella's crumpled forehead. I didn't see me opening the ring box the wrong way round, nor the curl of a lip when I presented it properly. I'm not sure what I did picture, but it wasn't this and as soon as it is out of my mouth, I curse myself for not reading the flags better.

The woman I love is slinging limp insults and damp socks at me. She accuses me of *craving performative heteronormativity,* and I wonder how a woman who couldn't say *reflection* earlier can spit the phrase with perfect clarity now.

Forty minutes later and she's slammed the door and I'm crying into a teacup filled with gin.

They put the arrest in the papers. It's on the news, too. The dad wasn't even in town that weekend, it just took them a while to figure that out.

Just a quiet fishing weekend, he said. *Myall Lakes.* He shakes his head and blinks like a startled vole. *Too awful.*

There are pictures of a boy lurching towards adulthood, an innocuous name, a fish eyed mother at his side. School mate of the boy. Had some beef about damage to a car and took a lighter to a pile of deadwood outside the son's room.

I just wanted to frighten him, the boy allegedly wept to the arresting officer.

The son holds it together by his father's side. *Now my boy's got no mum,* says the father, and he has to poke a fat dirty thumb into an eye socket. *It's just not fair.*

I wonder if Gis is watching the same news report, wonder if she's still filled with the impotent rage against the man, the machine, the mechanics of it all.

We haven't seen one another since the row: just two cold texts suggesting, without irony, that we *consciously uncouple* tell me that she didn't walk out of my house and into a truck. The friends that suggested we should meet are underwater-quiet.

While some other whisky-scorched tongue licks Gisella's neck, down the hill, I burn. I sit in a chair in front of the TV while hungry orange flames and the acrid smoke of *could-have-beens* take me alive.

NELSON'S GRAVE

GLYN MATTHEWS

My mother stopped at traffic lights. I fidgeted in the back. I didn't like the look of the man on the bike next to us. He had a bristly chin, and I could see right up his nostrils. He had a face like a cartoon eagle. His cycle helmet made him look even more dangerous. He looked down at me and I turned my eyes quickly away. I willed the lights to change and, at last, we accelerated. As we passed the cyclist I pulled out my tongue. The traffic slowed to a crawl and a quick glance revealed the cyclist coming up behind. I slithered out of my seatbelt and lay in the footwell.

"What on earth are you doing down there, Oliver?"

"I thought I saw a pound coin but it's a piece of silver paper."

"Get up at once and sit properly. And do up your seatbelt. Do you want me to break the law?"

We gathered speed and I breathed a sigh of relief as the eagle on a Raleigh disappeared behind us. In the rear-view mirror I could see a section of my mother's hair like a random piece of jigsaw, one of those annoying pieces you keep going back to, wondering where the heck they fit. More lights and the parcel beside me rocked slightly as we stopped. A woman in a white hatchback pulled up in the lane alongside. From my shorts pocket I retrieved the piece of paper I had hidden there, unfolded it and held it flat against the glass. I had written in bold felt-tipped capitals:

HELP – I'VE BEEN KIDNAPPED

She saw it and did a double-take. We pulled away and the woman slotted in behind us. I may have had a result. To make sure, I chanced a quick flash of my message through the rear window without my mother noticing.

The indicator t-tick, t-tick, t-ticked and we slowed to turn left and the hatchback braked behind us, I mouthed, 'help' at the woman and she raised her eyebrows. I gave her a suitably desperate look and raised my hand as if I was drowning. 'If that doesn't do it, nothing will,' I thought. We entered a road leading into a new housing estate. The lady in the hatchback carried on along the main road. I'd done all I could. I hoped for the best. I turned my attention to our surroundings. The houses were detached, those boring ones they build on 'desirable' estates these days with Lego front doors and hardly any front garden. They all look the same and they all have matching BMWs parked outside on Sundays.

The car stopped, my mother got out, flung open the rear door and dragged me out.

"Come on, hurry up, I'm double parked. And bring that parcel and mind the wrapping."

I fumbled with my seatbelt, and she reached impatiently

inside, taking the wind out of me as she leaned on my stomach while she released the catch.

"Ahhh, now look what you've made me do. I've broken my bloody nail."

"Mummy, you shouldn't swear."

"I'll swear if I bloody well want to."

"I'm just saying."

Oh, those perfect nails. She cares more for them than me. I reached for the parcel and dragged it after me. I noticed there were balloons tied to an ornamental tree and bright triangular flags hanging on a string across the front bay window spelling out 'happy birthday'. In her hurry to bundle me up the drive my mother almost knocked over a girl I didn't recognise, wearing a pink party dress. Yuck. In fact I didn't recognise any of the other children gabbling in the porch. I scanned the boys, looking for familiar faces but I was disappointed. They all looked too clean. Maybe there was somebody I knew inside.

My mother wrenched the parcel from my hands and thrust it at the lady who was welcoming the guests.

"Here, take this," she said, "I'm double parked."

Without a goodbye she pushed me forward and click-clacked across the pavement in her high-heels. How she drives in them I've no idea. My dad says she's 'death on wheels'. But he should talk, got done by the same speed camera twice in one day. Anyway here I am. Let's get that party started.

"Go through," said the lady who was collecting the gifts, giving me an odd look as I ducked beneath her arm and followed the sound of voices. I entered a living room full of unfamiliar children. I couldn't even see Andrew, the birthday boy. Still, it was quite a crush. Apparently, he had a lot of friends I didn't know. I was quite surprised. I wouldn't have said he was that popular. The boys had gathered more or less at one end of the room and the girls at the other. Standard procedure. I'm surprised there were any girls. Maybe Andrew's parents had hired them. Anyway, I stood at the edge of the boy brigade. I was ignored and I couldn't be bothered to say anything, so I wandered over to the girls. The one my mother tried to trample into the drive turned and smiled and said, "I'm Charlotte." She had a gap between her front teeth, a quite attractive feature but I wasn't going to say so. But I did try to make polite conversation. I looked at her incisors and was careful not to make any rabbit jokes. Instead, I smiled back and complimented her, "Hello, I'm Oliver," I said. "I expect you can spit right across a road through those teeth?"

She closed her mouth and turned back to the girls. A little rude, but I can take rejection. With parents like mine I've had plenty of practice.

A lady came into the room and clapped her hands and said how lovely it was to see us all. She said we shouldn't be shy and, to break the ice, we would play Musical Statues. We had to dance about and then freeze when the music stopped. And if you moved you were out. I jigged about like an idiot. I mean, you might as well when you get the chance. It's called 'getting in to the spirit', which is more than I can say for some of the others. Some of them should have been disqualified for hardly moving. That's cheating if you ask me and I was out well before the end. Not that I was bothered. I sat at the side and watched Charlotte twiddling about in her pink dress. She was taking it very seriously and was last in and won a packet of Gummy Bears. Next, we played Pass the Parcel which is one of the most boring party games ever invented. Charlotte won again. The prize was a pencil sharpener. Still, it's a useful lesson in the management of expectation.

Then the woman, who must have been Andrew's mother, set up a table with various items, hidden under a cloth and things got a bit more interesting.

"Now," she said, "We are going to play Nelson's Grave."

A hand shot up. "Please, what's Nelson's Grave?" a voice asked. It was Charlotte again.

"On this table are some of the mortal remains of Admiral Nelson."

"Please Miss, what's mortal remains, Miss?" asked a boy wearing a tie on a piece of elastic.

Who invited him? I helped him out, "Dead bits."

"Dead bits?"

"Yeah, like bones and brains and intestines and such. I saw a poodle get run over once and its guts sprayed out all over some kid in a pushchair eating an ice-cream. Made a right mess. Anyway, that's mortal remains, but of a dog."

"I don't want to play this game," said Charlotte.

"It's all right, it's just a game," the woman told her. And she pressed on with her prepared introduction, trying hard to get back on track. She cleared her throat and smiled, "Nelson's body was dug up by an archaeologist friend of mine and he has donated some of the body parts especially for this party and you will be allowed to examine them. But some items are very delicate and may crumble with exposure to light, so you will have to feel them carefully in the dark. Other bits are a bit gooey, some of his innards for instance."

"Don't say I didn't warn you," I interrupted.

"Nelson is one of our greatest heroes," she continued bravely, "so it is wonderful to be able to examine his remains.

Now, form a queue. We are going to turn the lights off and, one by one, you are going to come forward and feel different parts of his body."

"I want to go home," wailed Charlotte.

"Of course you don't, Charlotte," said Andrew's mother. "We haven't had tea yet."

"I don't want tea. I want my mummy."

"Shush now Charlotte. I'm sure you'll enjoy it when it comes to your turn."

Lights were extinguished and the queue became a conveyor of quailing, shrieking children shuddering at thought of dismembered body parts. Charlotte tried to stay at the back of the queue but was forced constantly to the front. I made sure of that.

"And this is a piece of Nelson's tongue – eyeball – rotting brain – earlobe – toe bone…"

And so it went on.

"And this is his blood. A bit congealed but never mind. Have a feel then lick your fingers…. if you dare."

"I'm going to be sick," said Charlotte.

The game over and the carpet cleaned, we sat around the dining table facing mounds of scrambled egg and fish paste sandwiches and finally, blancmange. Some diners seemed strangely quiet and picky but I dived in. I had two helpings of blancmange. There was a plate of chocolate fingers, great for dipping into the blancmange so I grabbed a handful. I don't need asking twice.

It was the best party I'd been to for ages though God knows whose birthday it actually was. The boy blowing out candles on the cake certainly wasn't Andrew. In fact, he pointed at me and asked his mother who I was. Cheek.

As the guests thinned out and were collected, to be taken home by grateful parents, I was asked to stand to one side in the hall. I hadn't nicked anything apart from some chocolate fingers for later, so I wasn't too bothered.

Eventually my mother came. She simply smiled without saying anything, ushered me out and shoved me into back of the car. Pulling into traffic she told me over her shoulder, it was a mistake anyone could make. What were the chances of there being two children's parties on the same road on the same day? She said all parties are much the same, so I hadn't missed much.

By the time we pulled out of the estate, it was spitting with rain and going dark. I sat back and watched the shadows cast by streetlights revolve around the car's interior. It had been a better day than I'd expected, though I didn't admit it to my mother, why spoil the upper hand, and I sat quietly munching chocolate fingers behind her back.

When we arrived home, it got even better – there was a police car with flashing lights parked outside and two police officers standing in the rain talking to my dad on the doorstep.

"What on earth do they want?" said my mother to herself.

I could have offered a guess, but I didn't want to spoil what was coming next.

LIMBO

CHRISSY PELUOLA

Ben didn't think he had done anything wrong, but it seemed like his body did. Something his nerves knew. It had been nine years, and the pacing of his heart could still override his sleep.

———

The first time, the fiftieth time, it didn't seem to matter.

"When the baby comes out, they won't be breathing," Ben warned the new doctor who was shadowing him. They were both wearing blue scrubs. It was three in the afternoon and Ben's scrubs were streaked with the dark smears of previous deliveries. He checked the new doctor's badge for a second time, reminding himself of her name: Mariella. They waited under the operating theatre's stage-lighting, minding the trolley they would use to resuscitate the baby. Despite her freckles, Mariella looked like Ben a few months ago, too much white around her pupils, neck muscles straining against pale skin, there was a tautness to her.

One of Mariella's long, black hairs had curled into a spiral on the white towels of the trolley. A heater hung over the trolley and warmed the towels. Ben held his latex-blue hands under it, feeling the heat gradually spread over his gloved knuckles. He always worried he would lift the newborn too high against the burning filaments of the trolley's heater. Did it take a certain kind of person or a certain kind of training to tolerate this, he wondered. Could you train soldiers out of PTSD?

"Why does she have to be knocked out?" asked Mariella, eyeing the very pregnant woman on the angled bed in the middle of the room.

The woman warily cradled her tummy with slim arms as the theatre staff milled around her. Her thin hospital gown tented over her swollen belly, pulling tight enough to mark out her belly button.

"She had a bad reaction to some of the drugs in the past, so she can't have an epidural to numb the area," Ben told the new doctor.

The mother ran her hands over the thick plait of hair running over her shoulder.

"Is that why the baby's dad isn't here?" asked Mariella, watching the mother's every move.

"No relatives allowed when the mother is unconscious," said a young midwife, who was lining a see-through cot with a roll of blue paper, smoothing it over the edges of the basin. Ben debated whether to tell Mariella that they usually only knocked the mother out in emergencies. The kind where the baby was going to die or get brain damage in the time it took to get an epidural in. Today the planned Caesarean section should be good preparation for Mariella, decided Ben, she could learn what to do when it wasn't an emergency. Once Mariella had been supervised at four deliveries, she would need to handle things alone. Backup would be a phone call and two storeys away.

It was Ben's second year of working as a doctor. He had seen more emergencies than he would have liked on this placement, always at night, when every alarm on the ward was whirring. Within a minute, the labouring patient had their bed rails rammed into place. There was no waiting for porters to come. With four sets of hands on the bed frame, the mother would be launched up the corridors at a run, with the team trying not to smack the bed or the mother's legs on their course. There were sets of double doors, corners and fire extinguishers to haul stiff wheels round.

Whilst the labour ward surgeons scrubbed their hands over wide metallic sinks, the baby doctor controlled what they could control: the arrangement of the towels, the pressures on the face mask, the height of the trolley. With the mother's prayers silenced by anaesthetic, the baby doctor and the midwife would be the ones willing the baby to life. The job of a baby doctor was to stand vigil as the unborn's oxygen levels trickled downwards, resisting the tension as the seconds ran into minutes. Their turn would come.

A lifeless baby wasn't like a rag doll. Their arms were too substantial, with their skin pulled firm over the nook of the elbow. At once, too solid and too floppy. Mariella and the other new doctors didn't know that yet, but they would soon. Then perhaps they would find, as Ben had, that the thought of mint-green corridors would drive their heartbeat surging into their ears.

"The drugs the mum gets, the baby gets too, so the baby will be knocked out at first," Ben explained.

"Knocked out knocked out?" asked Mariella.

"The anaesthetic should only last a minute or two, but we need to breathe for the baby until they are breathing for themselves," said Ben.

The Caesarean was progressing fast. Blue curtains were dropped around the firm mound of the patient's tummy. Over this, polythene covered every surface of the mother. Two surgeons either side, faceless in masks and caps steadily exposed the womb as rivulets of blood trickled into the covers' gutters.

The surgeons had made a hole in the womb. On either side, they pushed two bent fingers in and leant back with their full weight, stretching open an entrance. Mariella couldn't keep the alarm off her face. The theatre staff leaned back on their heels, disinterested.

"Are you okay to give the baby the breaths once the baby's out?" asked Ben.

Giving a nod, Marielle pulled her gloves taught against her fingers.

Sliding a hand into the womb's entrance, the surgeon cupped a hand under the baby's face and eased it out. Gripping the baby's blood-matted face, the surgeon wrangled a small shoulder and arm free. Small gushes of clear liquid emptied out the womb after each part of the baby. There was no waiting now. The gelatine cord was split in a single cut, releasing a spurt of blood that rolled over the mother. Within seconds the baby was being sped across the theatre in the cot towards them.

Ben didn't like the way the baby lolled in the hard plastic

cot, arms flopping out straight, no bend. As he lifted the bowed back and tiny legs onto the trolley, he reminded himself that babies were always floppy at first with a general anaesthetic.

"This is normal," said Ben firmly.

Using towels that had been laundered coarse, they quickly rubbed the baby clean of the gunk that caked each fold, over the chest, the soft belly, the creases of the eyes, the roll of the arms, the sticky helmet of fine damp hair. There was no cry, no gasp, no fluttering of the chest.

"The baby's not breathing. Time to start the breaths," said Ben.

With two shaky hands, Mariella cocooned the baby's face with the rubber mask, counting the breaths that Ben gave with a mouthed one-two-three. The baby's skin was faintly yellow in the trolley's beam. When Mariella lifted the mask, it left a white rim of pressure around the mouth. There was no response from the baby.

"And again," said Ben, noticing that the baby's arm stayed where it fell, no bend, no flex.

On the monitor, the baby had no heartbeat. Ben's eyes kept flicking back to the monitor, but there was no beep and no wave. The monitor wasn't detecting a pulse. This wasn't supposed to happen. General anaesthetic wasn't supposed to do this.

Pushing the end of his stethoscope onto the baby's small chest, he listened. Under the harsh whoosh of air forcing its way, the faint tapping of a heart was just audible. It was beating too slowly. Mariella was frozen in concentration, gripping the mask to the baby's face. After five long breaths, the newborn hadn't roused himself.

The monitor still wasn't detecting much of a heartbeat. Ben lifted the baby's arm and let it drop, noting its limp fall. He could feel his own heartbeat pounding through his chest now.

"Is this normal?" asked Mariella, her eyes wide with fear. Ben didn't reply. The baby's skin looked pale, but his eyelids were dusky. The sensor was only recording intermittently. Airway, breathing, heart rate, Ben recited to himself, focusing on the steady rhythm of breaths he was giving to the baby. The midwife continued rubbing each limb, tousling energy into them. The monitor was starting to detect a heartrate- lethargic beats that were far too slow. Panic reared in Ben, as his grip on control slipped away.

Steeling his tone, Ben suggested he take over holding the mask now. He felt the squishy plastic in his grip and pressed it to the baby's face.

Turning to one of the theatre staff he said, 'Bleep my registrar. Please.'

The theatre team had started to realise that something bad was unfolding on the baby trolley. Staff edged closer, craning their necks to see beyond the huddle that surrounded the baby. Across the room, the unconscious mother dredged through darkness as they struggled to keep her baby this side of life. A few corridors away, the new father waited, checking the football scores on his phone.

Sweat beaded at Ben's temples in the waves of heat radiating from the trolley's heater. The midwife stood at his shoulder; her skin glowing in the gleam of the red-hot filaments.

"Have either of you ever given chest compressions to a baby before?" Ben asked, clamping the mask against the baby's cheeks.

"No," said the midwife.

"Only on a doll," said Mariella.

Ben hoped his senior would be fast.

Despite the breaths, the oxygen levels weren't improving. The heartrate was still low.

"Time to start chest compressions," he nodded at the midwife, "I'll keep the breaths going."

"Now?"

"Now."

Taking two fingers like a gun, the midwife jabbed them into the middle of the baby's chest. The chest plunged and rebounded with each thrust. The midwife's braids sprung around as her head rocked with each jab, eyes intent on the centre of the small chest. She looked at Ben. He nodded in response. Ben kept looking to the doors, hoping to see his senior walk through them. The baby's eyelids glanced backwards to reveal glassy unseeing eyes. No-one is coming to save you, he realised.

Ben turned up the pressure on his mask and started giving more forceful breaths. Again and again, they pushed air in and let it flow out. He listened again to the heart's faltering patter. Adjusting the face mask, he squeezed the baby's jaw towards it, feeling the firm resistance of the baby's cheeks and mouth under his hands.

"Any minute now," he told Mariella.

There was one thing he hadn't tried yet.

"Can someone pass me the laryngoscope?" he asked.

"What does it look like?" asked Mariella.

Ben tried to describe the laryngoscope's metal handle and the long-curved edge, whilst he gripped the mask. The midwife threw the drawer of the trolley open and rummaged through. Using the sleeve of his top, Ben wiped the sweat trickling into his eye. Standing upright again, the midwife held an instrument aloft that looked like a curved metal claw.

With a shaking hand, Ben removed the face mask, slipped the curved edge of the laryngoscope over the baby's tongue, and pulled the jaw upwards to see the vocal cords. The dark tunnel of the baby's throat was frothy with bubbles. As he tried to suction the bubbles out, the baby started to gag. The gag turned into a cough and then a weak cry. Startled hopeful, Ben pulled the laryngoscope out and watched. The midwife rubbed the baby with towels, urging him on. The mother slept on in her narcotic void. As the three of them hung over the baby, his fists started to clutch at his palms and his chubby knees drew in towards his belly. The baby's cries became more forceful, as his face scrunched and reddened. Ben's legs trembled as relief and adrenaline washed over him.

He couldn't wait for this rotation to be over.

ONLY ONE MAN DIED

DENARII PETERS

"Don't worry. He won't get stuck. He practised that manoeuvre only last week."

"Who said I was worried? Dan knows what he's doing."

If Dan's mother wasn't concerned, everyone else in the room was. Besides, the way she stabbed at those potatoes gave the lie to her words.

I'd been in this kitchen when Dan was practising. He'd taken two upright dining chairs and placed their seats one in front of the other, then slithered beneath the crossbar, through the back of the first one – a space less than twelve inches square – across the seats and through the gap at the other side, twisting so he landed on his feet. He was ever so slender but even so it should not have been possible.

"He dislocates his hips," said Ros, the sister proud of her elder brother's ability.

Dan and his sibling Richard were members of the Craven cave rescue team. It was the end of one of the longest, hottest summers in living memory but that afternoon the weather had broken. Lightning flashed around Morecambe Bay and raindrops cascaded down. The squall came out of nowhere. Clouds formed in an instant and the road outside became a river.

The call when it came had been expected. Dan had already stowed his gear, so it lay ready in a rucksack by the door. Weekend cavers are not always as careful as they should be. The hot weather had lured many inexperienced potholers into difficulty during the long summer season. Those had been easy rescues: a broken ankle or a couple separated from the rest of their team but having the sense to go no deeper and soon recovered. If someone was in trouble in this weather, any rescue would be nothing like as straightforward as those.

The family did not have a telephone. Instead a Land Rover pulled up outside to collect Dan. Richard couldn't go. He had injured his leg playing football a few days before.

As soon as Dan had left, his mother started on the potatoes. They would be baked ready for his return as he was bound to be cold, wet and tired.

I was only a guest at the house. I suggested it was time I left but Mrs Ellwood shook her head. Ros had invited me. I was supposed to be staying the night. "Besides, I wouldn't send a dog out on..." Her voice trailed away.

Richard brought out a large hand drawn map of the cave system beneath Gaping Gill. He spread it over the kitchen table. I didn't understand how he thought this would help but his father, who had been sitting silent in his armchair by the Aga, came across and the two of them began tracing routes through tunnels and caverns.

It would take at least forty-five minutes to reach the cave system. Then the team would have to walk some distance over rough terrain. The rescue could well take all night and still the rain continued to fall, the streams to rise, the danger to increase.

"They'll be on the A683 by now."

"No, Dad, they'll have taken the A6. It's longer but they'll get there quicker by that road." Richard stood beside his father, one grey head and one with straggly black hair bent together over the diagram.

Forty minutes later they agreed the rescue team would have reached the limit of the terrain the Land Rover could handle. They would have to leave the vehicle, each loaded with ladders, lights, spare bulbs and batteries.

"For every hour someone travels through a system, it takes the rescuers at least twelve to get them out again. And that's if they're only a bit lost. If they're injured, you're looking at a full day," said Richard without looking up.

Beyond the window the rain kept on falling, a drenching curtain so thick you could see nothing beyond it. Up around Gaping Gill the ground would have been hard and dry only hours before but now it would be a sea of sticky mud concealing sharp shards of slippery stone. The waterfalls in those caves were some of the biggest drops in the British Isles. Through the drought they would have been trickles but now they would be torrents. The change in the weather had been so sudden, flooding would be inevitable.

Richard traced a path on the map. "They could have gone in through Rat Hole, taken the old east passage to Mud Hall and Car Pot..." His finger became still. "...or they might have headed for Far Waters. There are some pretty tight squeezes on the way, even for our Dan."

"Maybe, or they could have entered by Corky's Pot then gone on to Disappointment Pot, though I hope not. There's bound to be a lot more water that way."

There was a loud hiss from the Aga, as though a bucketful of rainwater had found its way down the chimney. The flames dipped and a sudden coldness came into the room.

"Get some more wood, will you, love?"

Mrs Ellwood opened the fire chamber while Ros and I headed for the tiny room next to the kitchen that held the fuel.

We gathered up handfuls of tinder dry sticks and, hugging our bounty close to us, we returned and fed the fire. The door was closed, and warmth was restored.

Ros remained on her feet. "We're getting a bit low, Ma."

"We'll be fine. We'll sort it in the morning."

"No, I'd like a bit of air. I'll go out and find a few more branches." It was a ridiculous idea. The hedges on the opposite side of the hill would be spattered in mud and the trees would be sodden, their branches bent over under the weight of falling water. One wet twig would be enough to drown the flames of the warning, welcoming Aga. But I understood. She could not sit and listen to the two men discussing Dan's possible fate. He might be diving, forced to swim through an underground tide in bitter cold conditions, all the time surrounded by pitch darkness.

Outside in our own darkness, we tramped along, our heads bent, Ros dragging her little trolley behind her, its wheels slipping on the slick surface. We took the path round the side of the castle, past the priory church and on into the gloom. There were no street lights. The path was a narrow, descending cart track between steep sloping fields. The trolley kept catching its wheels among the stones and turning over. Reaching out to steady it, I slipped and skidded, falling into the clinging, sticky mud. We were so wet we might as well have been drowning under a waterfall.

We turned back. At least there were no narrow rock walls to compress our lungs, no twisting tunnels in which to lose our way. But without warning we were tramping through a torrent which had not been there only minutes before. We were forced to abandon the trolley.

Yet still the rain and the lightning persisted. Our shoes filled with mud. We were getting tired.

Ros muttered, "Exposure. Cavers die of exposure more often than drowning."

But she and I were in no danger. We were no more than ten minutes from Ros's home. Yet in the darkness behind the priory, with no light and with water clutching at us, threatening to drag us down, I had never been so afraid.

As my teardrops joined the raindrops, ahead reared a black shadow: the imposing bulk of the priory. We reached the stone wall surrounding it, using it to trace our way forward, frozen fingers trailing through moss more like seaweed, over snails more like barnacles and through nettles whose leaves were too sodden to sting.

We rounded the corner. Across the shimmering water between the kerbs, swirling around the overflowing drains, lay our route to safety, to shelter. Splashing across this wider, though shallower, river, we arrived back at her door and tumbled inside, filling the hallway with our damp presence, for an instant forgetting Dan, the caves and the danger. We laughed at our bedraggled reflections in the ancient, tarnished mirror.

In the kitchen no-one was speaking and our laughter was cut short. Ros's parents and brother clustered round the radio. The authorities had just issued a severe weather warning. No-one was to venture out unless they had to. The A6 was closed due to a crash involving several cars. It was feared a couple of hikers were lost out on the moors. There was no mention yet of any lost cavers.

The rain stopped but we did not celebrate. Richard estimated the lower reaches of the Gaping Gill system would be filled with water and there would be no sudden end to the flow. He pointed to several underground streams criss-crossing the map. All of them would have burst their banks. No dry refuge anywhere.

Ros's mother removed the shrivelled, over-cooked potatoes from the oven and threw them away. No-one was hungry. She took fresh ones from a basket, stabbed them deep into their cores and placed them in the Aga.

It was almost midnight but no-one suggested we got any sleep.

Yet sleep I did. The room was warm and my own concerns were not as all enveloping as a sister's worry or a parent's fear.

I woke to a pale dawn, light streaming in through the windows. The scent of fresh bread had replaced the background smell of baking potatoes. This family had their routines and in routine there is always solace. Fear is diminished when faced with familiarity.

Dan had been away for over fifteen hours. There had been no word. The radio talked of casualties from the accident on the A6 then interrupted itself with a breaking story about the two hikers now rescued from the fells. No mention of Gaping Gill.

Richard began to fret. "Why does no-one come? Someone from cave rescue should have brought us news by now even if..."

Outside the window, the sky was a clear, mocking blue. The sun was already warm enough to dry the road but it would take many hours before waters underground would recede.

An hour later the sound of a car arriving was followed by a knock.

As Ros opened the door, we all saw the police car and heard her shout out as she let the visitors in.

Exhausted, soaking wet and draped in a thick, grey blanket, Dan followed her inside.

The policeman was a step behind them. "Bit of a hero, your boy, Mrs Elwood. Saved a baby. Never seen anything like it."

"A baby? Someone took a baby into the caves?"

"What? Nothing to do with caves. No, this was the A6. Ten or so cars all piled up. We couldn't reach the baby, but your Danny did. Like an eel, he was, straight through the passenger window of one car, over the back seat, through that window and into the next. Ripped his coat to shreds on the broken glass but he brought the child out."

"Shame I could do nothing for the driver."

"He was beyond help. But it's thanks to you, Danny boy, and the rest of your team helping out till the ambulances got through that only one man died."

The policeman gone, Richard tapped the map. "What about the cavers?"

"Huh, we got news of them just as we finished up helping the police. They committed the ultimate sin, that lot, the only one for which a caver can never be forgiven. Before they set out they left plenty of messages, told people when to expect them back and when to begin to worry. Only they never did reach Gaping Gill. The closest they got was the Square and Compass in Clapham. The only liquid they encountered was best Yorkshire Ale."

THEY THINK IT'S ALL OVER

COLIN ROTE

30th July 1966 is one of those dates, for boys of my generation, when everybody remembers where they were. A bit like when President Kennedy was shot, although I was never actually able to remember where I was for that. For most boys, the date was memorable because the England football team won the World Cup. But, for me, it was an unforgettable date for another reason.

I'd never had much interest in football. Our school played rugby, and the games master referred to football as a game played by hooligans. Prior to 1966, I didn't even know there was such a thing as the World Cup, but having it played in England fired up the media and consequently the public, so by the time the tournament started, everyone was aware of it, and at school, you were nobody if you couldn't recite the names of the entire team. So I learned them.

I watched the game at Ian Jackson's house. Jackson (we all knew each other by surnames at school) had been a fellow sixth former until we took our 'A' levels in June. His house was preferred for two reasons: because it had, undisputedly, the largest television of any of the parents' houses; and because Jackson had a dad who told all the boys to call him Dave and let them have a glass of beer from his Watney's Party Seven can. He was a builder and more approachable by far than other parents at the boys' grammar school; the solicitors, accountants, civil servants and so on. Jackson had been useless at maths, and I got to be an insider in his circle by regularly letting him copy my homework, a strategy that got Jackson through the school year but failed him at exam time, much to his parents' puzzlement. Even though Jackson dropped maths in sixth form, I was deemed to have done enough over the years to stay on the periphery of the preferred group.

The day hadn't started well. My father insisted I wear a shirt and tie for the visit, which would have been an even greater disaster if I hadn't begged him to drop me at the end of the road where Jackson lived. As soon as Dad's car pulled away, I slid the tie off, rolled it up, and put it in my pocket. I still faced a barrage of ridicule as I arrived dressed in a formal shirt, open at the collar, and grey flannel trousers. They were all dressed in jeans or corduroys.

"Come for a day at the office, old boy?" Dave said, in what he imagined to be a posh accent, and ruffled my hair as though I was eleven.

I can still remember bits of the match, a grainy black-and-white image on the screen, despite Dave having closed the curtains to make the room more like a cinema. I especially remember the end, when Geoff Hurst collected a long pass, high up the pitch on his own, to the sound of Kenneth Wolstenholme's voice commentating the soon-to-be immortal words, "Some people are on the pitch. They think it's all over."

Hurst shot for goal, the West German goalkeeper didn't even dive as the ball cannoned into the net, and Wolstenholme intoned, "It is now."

The joy after the match led to the opening of another Party Seven, and, even though it was a dull day, the revelry spilled out into the garden. The 'hip' lads lit up and collogued by the shed. I hadn't learnt to smoke and wasn't going to try in such a large public arena, so I moped uncomfortably, hands in pockets, by the dustbin at the side of the house, too excited to walk home but too paralyzed by feelings of inferiority to join in.

After a while, Jackson's sister, a dark-haired girl who I had met before but never really taken any notice of, emerged out of the back door of the house, next to the dustbin.

"They won then," she said, stopping next to me. I felt a blush flow into my cheeks, not because I wasn't used to talking to girls, although I wasn't, but because I might be seen talking to her by the others, especially Jackson.

"Yes, four, two."

"You'd think they'd won the war again, the way everyone's carrying on." I looked down and smiled. "Silly, if you ask me, twenty-two grown men chasing a bag of wind around a field." I snorted with laughter. If she were a member of the debating society at school, I would have accused her of reductio ad absurdum, but it struck me as having a core of truth. I looked up at her, and she was smiling, showing a set of small white teeth, all even apart from her left canine, which was out of line with the others—not a snaggle tooth exactly, not as severe as that—just overlapping the tooth in front a little, a tiny imperfection in an otherwise perfect smile. I thought that imperfection made her the most beautiful girl I'd ever seen. My chest felt light, and there was a stirring in the pit of my stomach.

"Don't let your brother hear you say that," I said, catching her eye, which was dark and mischievous.

"He never listens to anything I say. Boys don't listen, they tell. They tell you a football player they'd never heard of three weeks ago is the best footballer in the world, just because a posh bloke on the telly says so. And next month it'll be a racing driver, or an astronaut, or something. Something they wish they could be." I felt chastened. I recognized what she said in the prattle that passed for conversation between the boys; half parroting so-called experts and the other half wishful thinking. "Bobby Charlton should have scored from that range; I could have done it in my sleep."

"You don't like boys, then?" I said it with a smile and surprised myself that I was capable of teasing. Was that what flirting is?

"Most of them are idiots. Some are okay." She shifted her weight, dropping a hip, and her slim body shape changed from one set of curves to another.

I wanted to stare at those curves and study the way they intersected to produce a configuration so fascinating.

"Are you one of the ones going to university?"

"Yeah, I hope so; it depends on my grades."

"What subject?"

"Civil Engineering."

"What's that?" She wrinkled her nose.

"Building things."

"Like my Dad? You don't need a university degree to do that." She flicked her bobbed hair, and I watched the arc of its swirl.

"No. Really big things like bridges, motorways, that sort of thing."

"Do you really think you could do something like that?"

"Yes, I think so. Obviously, I'd be starting at the bottom." She shifted from one hip to the other and her A-line dress slid up her leg. I tried not to look, but I failed and hoped she didn't notice. She stepped closer to me, and I could smell her perfume. I drew a sharp breath. I could feel an erection starting and began to panic. If she saw, or worse, if any of the boys saw, the shame would be unbearable. My chest burned. 'I'm sorry, I can't remember your name.' As soon as I said it, I felt the heat in my face double.

"Helen," she said, "you're Peter, aren't you?"

————

The evening set in, and still the boys relived the victory along with Dave, who sometimes crushed Jackson into his side in a show of affection my dad would have deemed vulgar, as toast after toast was made to Alf Ramsey and the boys. They told each other, in great detail over and over, how the win was achieved until it was hard to believe they had all witnessed it together.

Around the corner of the house, Helen and I talked about the future. She was confident and realistic. She had taken her 'O' levels and had a place at a teacher training college in town, if she got her grades. I shared my anxiety about not getting the two As and a B needed for Uni.

By the time Helen's Mum called her, she was leaning against the wall alongside me, our arms pressed against each other's. I was amazed by the fact I was touching a real girl and thrilled and fascinated by the feel of her. I was wondering if I should take her by the hand.

The call made her jump, and the motion caused me to jerk my arm away. There was an urgency about the tone of Helen's Mum's voice, and in the way Helen trotted to the door in response. I braced myself in case I was about to be on the receiving end of a rebuke about my conduct. But, to my surprise, what actually happened was Helen walked back towards me with her head down. Only when she was standing directly in front of me did she look up. There were tears in her eyes.

"There are some people here to pick you up."

"My parents?" Why would they come to pick me up? They weren't expecting me home yet, and in any case, it would be mortifying for my father to come here.

"No. Mr. and Mrs. Gough? They said they're your next-door neighbours."

I couldn't fathom a credible reason why they were here asking for me. I must, somehow, be in deep trouble, but I couldn't think how or why.

"It's about your Dad; they said he's died." The meaning of the words didn't register fully. I felt distant, as though I were watching the real world on a screen, like Dave's big television, and I was an observer rather than a participant. "Peter?"

"My dad?"

"Yes," she was fully crying now, and Dave came running across, face full of concern for his daughter.

I came back into the real world with a jolt at the thought that it was just my luck this would happen when I was talking properly to a girl for the first time. That this was my first thought upon learning of my father's death didn't seem at all strange to me at the time.

Helen's Mum whispered something in Dave's ear and then

came over and hugged me to her. And I let myself be hugged, a thing that had almost never happened to me.

"It was his heart; he didn't suffer," said Mr. Gough, who was, by now, standing in the back doorway, tall and formal in his sports jacket. "We'd better get you home, your mother needs you."

But, in case I've misled you, it wasn't the death of my father that made the date memorable. Not directly, anyway. It was the aftermath.

As an only child, I felt it was my duty not to abandon my widowed mother just when she needed me, so I didn't go to university that year. The plan was for me to apply for the following year, but by then I was an apprentice Surveyor and also deeply in love with Helen, and she with me.

And so, fifty-eight years later, we are all in this hospital ward: Helen, me, and our adult children Michael, and Jenny, who is a Civil Engineer, as it happens. We were a proper 'happy-ever-after' family until this illness struck.

Now, I gaze at Helen and see past the lines that age has etched into her face, past the pallor and the looseness of her skin, and see the girl I met that day. Beautiful.

I look across at the children, faces wrought with anxiety and sorrow, and can't help but remember those words: 'They think it's all over'.

And as my final breath leaves my body, and the faces of those I love fade to grey, I hear God's voice say, "It is now."

THE DEEPEST PART OF MAN

JAMES SCHANNEP

September 13th, 1912. To the members of the press, the university faculty, and to family and friends: I release this letter with deepest regret, per my instructions. –JD Chapman

From: Sacnej Mensa, PhD
126 Essex St
Salem, MA 01970

May 31, 1912

To: Professor Jessen D Chapman
c/o Miskatonic University
1 Miskatonic Lane
Arkham, MA 01914

Dearest friend and colleague,

My forthcoming journey to Peru and the lost city of Machu

Picchu is well-known throughout my circles. However, my reasons for choosing this destination have hitherto remained unclear to all, including my travel companion. I am certain that my assertions will seem akin to madness, but as another with a scientific mind, I implore you to read on with the courtesy of belief interspersed with rational skepticism until the final declaration has been made.

I write to you as an admission of fact, though if all goes well and the mystery is revealed, I shall insist you burn this letter, never to share my dreadful account. I am sure you understand the need for discretion, so I'll stress that point for a second time: burn this letter should you hear from me again. I don't simply speak out of concern for my own reputation, but more for fear of the knowledge itself.

Some of the phrases herein—I dare not call them incantations, though that is what they certainly are—should remain unknown to the outside world. As you read these (and I cannot possibly state this with more importance), do not under any circumstances utter them aloud. I give you undue burden even by recording them, but they add verisimilitude to my account and we are both men who ply our trade in fact and the details found therein.

I'm afraid I've hesitated in telling this tale, perhaps leaning on word of warning to forestall the need to put the events to paper, but I shall do so no longer.

It all began a year prior to the planned date of my ascent to the mysterious citadel. I had a persistent vision, not quite a nightmare, although the experience left me with an odious sense of dread. This jilting hallucination, like a message replayed on phonograph, with grooves of memory etched deeper with each recitation, though none so clear as the original.

You see, Bingham had sent me samples from the excavation site, and I set to work at their translation. Despite my expertise, I found no culture known to man where the inscriptions would fit. There was a curious rhyme and rhythm to the phrases, even while their meanings remained elusive. They replayed within the amphitheater of my mind, over and over again, until the recitation gave rise to something…other.

My vision was extremely lucid. I could see myself, as if from an observer's perspective as I climbed. In the dead of night, always in the blackest hour, I found myself venturing up a moss-covered hill, its sickly green ooze slick beneath my boots. There was a chill in the air, and in the high altitude, I found it difficult to catch my breath, as if some wretched hand was clutching at my neck.

Still, like one with a singular sense of purpose, I pressed forward through the unfamiliar sounds of the jungle, uncon-cerned with whence I came or where I was going next. The moon was a bright specter, and my eyes played tricks on me. I could see ungainly shadows following my every move. In the form of this out-of-body experience, I wanted to warn myself, but found I had no external voice with which to do so.

Inexorably, I found the ruins, covered over with jungle growth, just like they were when Bingham reclaimed them. Though I'd only seen a few pictures of the ruins up to this point, I knew them by name. Only now did I find their presence within the landscape obtrusive, wrong in such a manner as an affront against nature. Their looming walls were painfully angled; their geometry defying the living surroundings to the point of nausea. My head spun because of some ancient power the ruins possessed, yet still I pressed onward to reach their pale, languid features.

A cavern suddenly opened near me—or rather, I felt as if it had always been there—and reached out to me with soul-gripping strength. The ubiquitous darkness extended beyond its mouth, like some great chasm that led straight to hell. Why I stepped forward, I cannot say.

My footfalls echoed with a cacophony of whispers and hushed laughter, so that each scuff of my soles on the hard, merciless stone reverberated like a devil within my ear. Water dripped down the walls in slow, tepid drops. It was as if the cave itself salivated at the prospect of devouring me as its meal.

The snickering and breathing sounds intensified, to the point where I had no recourse save to stop in my tracks, close my eyes, press my hands against mine ears, and hold my own breath. For a time, it worked, and there were no further sounds. Then, just as my lungs began to burn for want of air, it came like a cool breeze: *runajpata astawan…*

I froze, trying to grasp what I'd just heard. Was it a voice? A trick of the wind? As if in answer, it sounded again, this time as the completion of the phrase that I'd somehow known was unfinished.

…ukhuyninqa pataqaran.

Those ethereal tones, the eldritch, otherworldly rasp spewed forth at me and turned my bones to cold milk. I wasn't sure if the words had even been spoken aloud, or if the wretched foulness had originated within my own mind. Those ineffable words themselves, had been etched onto my consciousness the same way they might have been carved with hieroglyphs upon the ruins all around. 'Twas very the phrase I'd been obsessing over in my translation work.

That's when it hit me, with a kind of certainty that only occurs in dreams: the voice in question was mine.

At this dark revelation, I stepped toward myself from the shadows. That is to say, another me, a *doppelgänger*, moved in and enveloped me with a sinister embrace. In my forty-six years upon this earth, I've never experienced a night-terror such as this, and my own fright was palpable. Although, I'd be remiss not to reveal that I felt the grasp was one of longing, a horrible love that only phantasmagoria could offer. It was glad I'd come to this place. That I'd received its invitation, sent to me through space and time, and had heeded the call.

I looked upon my own countenance, yet this was no mirror. All of my features were cragged and wicked; there was a trace of youth in the indolent face, although most of it seemed somehow stolen. The eyes looked back at me with the same infinity as the cavern itself, a black, deathly emptiness. The lips parted, head fell back and mouth opened; the vapor that then spewed forth was one of lurid sulfur. The words that emerged were not uttered by this apparition, but instead were born in some otherworldly dimension not known to man. His form simply allowed their exit: *runajpata astawan ukhuyninqa pataqaran.*

As the words mixed with the imprintation upon my conscious-ness, my *other's* fingers pressed into my flesh. There was no pain as they moved through my skin and became my skin, his sallow glow taking over my own pale complexion. We merged, became one, but more than that, he overtook me, not with struggle or conflict, but much to my horror, I allowed him and *willed* him to possess and become me.

I couldn't scream out, or worse, I didn't want to. There was less of myself as he shifted into me; to be more accurate, he grew while I shrank. Like the sands in an hourglass sifting from one side to the other, I was pouring out and he was filling up. This wasn't an out-of-body experience at all, but a transfer-ence of body and soul.

Just as he replaced me, I awoke from my trance. Back home; transmission complete.

I'll spare you the rest of the planning details of my trek up to the Lost City of the Incas, of procuring a travel companion, porters and guides, and of arranging the rest of the particulars for my trip. Suffice it to say, I had to go. Something compelled me, and I cannot explain why.

I know it seems like madness to have a vision such as this and to succumb to the wishes of the fiend. Perhaps I could argue I must go there to conquer the vision, the fear that hovers over my every waking moment, but that wouldn't be entirely true. Yes, my rational mind says to expose the shadows to the light and erase them from the darkness, yet I fear it is I who might be erased.

The deep dread that I'll be lost upon my arrival is pervasive, and yet I can't alter this destiny that has been thrust upon me. My one fail-safe is this letter. It must be released after my planned date of return, September 12th, unless I return to you in person to instruct otherwise. Should I not return and ask you to burn it; to laugh at this cloying obsession and share with me the *Pisco* brandy of that land while we sit by your hearth and discuss my foolhardy safeguard as old friends, then you *must* release this letter.

For if I do not ask you to burn it, the inscrutable truth would be that it is not I, not truly, who has returned to you.

Fare thee well,

Sacnej Mensa

FINDING TREASURE

MICHELLE SHINN

'That's where our Emma walked for the first time, do you remember?'

Dennis pointed just past the paved ramp that led down to the beach, where some forty-something years ago their daughter had taken her first wobbly steps, turning to look at them both in wide-eyed astonishment before promptly falling on her bottom.

Joan followed his finger to the spot, then looked back at him, her mouth doing that opening and closing thing a couple of times before she lost interest, fiddling with a button on her blouse.

'Never mind, love,' he said, taking her arm and continuing their walk along the promenade. Triggering Joan's memories was like hunting for buried treasure. This beach was like a map with X's all around, you just had to know where to find them and start to dig.

Gorleston was special to them. They first started visiting when Emma was just a baby. Back then, you didn't board a plane for your holiday, you just hopped in the car and travelled to the coast. They had fallen in love with the small Norfolk seaside town, with its golden sandy beach, flanked by a wide promenade and backed by dramatic grassy cliffs.

Many a summer day had been spent here, building sandcastles, tossing frisbees, digging out pennies for the nearby arcade. Gorleston, like them, was a little tired around the edges now, but when they were deciding where to retire, they had both agreed this was the place.

They were nearing the bandstand, set back from the beach in a park, when he caught the dreamy notes of 'Moonlight Serenade'. Their song. It had been the first dance at their wedding, and they'd glided many a smooth foxtrot to it over the years. He steered them towards the sound, his confidence growing as Joan gripped his arm tighter. The brass band weren't quite the same as Glenn himself, but it was near enough. There, on the grass next to the bandstand, with kids kicking crisp amber leaves, and dogs of all shapes and sizes exploring the park with their noses, he hummed the tune in Joan's ear, and she leaned towards him, closing her eyes. Taking her in his arms, they began to dance. Their feet remembered the steps perfectly and he could almost imagine they were teenagers again on their first date.

They met when he was working as a driver, collecting deliveries from a sweet factory. Joan worked on the packing line, and he'd caught a glimpse of her one day when he was waiting for his truck to be loaded. A petite, curvy brunette, she was holding court with a circle of admirers enthralled by her storytelling. Her laugh was so wicked it made him hungry to hear it, desperate to be the one to elicit such a mesmerising sound. He began making excuses to hang around until she'd have her break, but it took him a few weeks to muster the courage to speak to her. The first time he asked her for a date she let him down gently. But after a few further failed attempts, he realised a special girl like her wouldn't be won so easily. He was sure she liked him too, she teased him relentlessly, always singling him out in the crowd.

The women on the line removed their shoes when they came to work to prevent them from being ruined, replacing them with plimsols provided by the factory. One day, he stole her best pair, shiny red Mary Janes, placing them high on the rafters and refusing to take them down until she agreed to a date. She had a glint in her eye when she said yes, saying it was the only way a funny looking chap like him would manage to get a girl.

Goose bumps prickled his arms as he inhaled the familiar vanilla notes of her perfume, the same one she'd always worn. This day felt special, the warmth of the sun on his back, the band playing this song. He drew back slightly to see her face. She opened her eyes, smiling up at him, and for a fleeting moment, he had her back. Returning her smile, he reached out to stroke her cheek, realising his mistake immediately as her face contorted into a frown.

'Who are you? Why am I here?' she shouted, pushing him away.

A mum wheeling a buggy nearby shot him a distrustful look. He nodded in her direction, raising a hand as if to say, I've got it under control.

'It's ok, love. It's me, Den.' He risked a step towards her.

'No, no,' she was shaking her head, backing away. Then she turned, striding towards the beach, rejoining the promenade. He made no attempt to catch her. It was for the best when she was like this. Instead, he followed at a distance, until her pace slowed and she turned full circle, peering around like an abandoned child. Eventually she sat down on a bench, folding her hands in front of her.

Purchasing two ice-creams from a nearby stall, he approached. 'I got you a ninety-nine Joanie.'

'Thanks Den,' she said, and the smile extended all the way to her eyes.

The world stopped. It was the first time she'd said his name in a year.

————

When the doctor first told them, it had been her that had comforted him, clasping him tightly while his whole body trembled as if he was outside in the snow in his underwear rather than the oppressively hot consultation room.

He'd teased her when she had mistakenly called their granddaughter Emma, or that time she phoned him confused about why she was in town, and he had to remind her about her hairdressers' appointment. Naively he assumed her memory loss was a consequence of age, nothing to worry about.

They'd discussed what to do as the disease progressed, and she had urged him to put her in a home if it became too much. 'I could never do that Joanie,' he'd said, kissing the rosy apples of her cheeks.

The doctor had said they could have years, but she wasn't one of the lucky ones. Within six months she was leaving the gas on, getting lost if she went out alone and even beginning to forget who he was.

Worse had been the moments of clarity. One time she had said she was going upstairs to lie down. It was unlike her to nap, and he'd followed a few minutes later. She had been staring at herself in the dressing-table mirror, as if trying to cling on to her own identity. As he approached the tears began to fall. She had begged him to not let Emma bring the grandchildren when she got worse, she couldn't bear the thought of not recognising them.

———

A light drizzle was in the air, and he turned up his face to meet it. Rising from the bench he extended his elbow.

'Shall we, madam?'

She beamed at him, clasping his arm, and they continued their walk. He let himself imagine that they were just a normal couple enjoying an afternoon stroll. He wasn't kidding himself though, since saying his name, she hadn't uttered another word, occasionally sneaking a glance at him as they meandered along, as if he was someone she'd known long ago she couldn't quite place.

The sprinkling of rain had cleared the beach of the majority of its occupants. Just a few brave souls with their windbreakers up remained. They were approaching a parade of shops that housed the arcades and a few tired-looking cafes.

'I'm hungry,' she blurted suddenly.

He realised he was also ready to eat, or maybe it was just the enticing vinegary tang wafting in their direction.

'Me too, Joanie.'

She gazed at him expectantly and he brushed a stray curl from her face.

'How about fish and chips?'

She nodded enthusiastically and he reached for her hand, searching her eyes first to check it was ok. Leading her to the cafe, he settled her down on one of the plastic chairs outside. The sun had peeped from behind a cloud, and it would be nicer to eat in the fresh air. She wasn't great in busy places these days.

'I'll only be a few minutes love – cod, chips and gravy, is it?'

'And a barmcake,' she said, licking her lips.

'And a barmcake then.' He risked a kiss on her forehead, letting his hand rest briefly on one of her shoulders.

The air was warm inside the cafe causing the windows to steam up. He used the sleeve of his jacket to rub a circle clear, peering out at her while he waited his turn. It was here he'd lost her last time. He'd only taken his eyes off her for a second. Hadn't realised he was still capable of running. After describing Joan to countless passersby, one had finally pointed to the cliffs overlooking the promenade. She was on the bench they used to frequent the winter they had first retired. The view of the beach was special up there, you could see for miles – from the pier right down to the pub where they'd sometimes treat themselves to dinner. She had risen when he had huffed to a stop in front of her, resting his hands on his knees to catch his breath. Her lips began to move but before she could form any words he had grabbed her by the shoulders, shaking her roughly.

'Don't you ever do that to me again, Joan. You hear me? *Never* again.'

All of the anxiety and fear gushed out, quickly overridden by guilt at her bewildered expression. Then a terrible sense of loss. Not only for what she might have been about to say, but for what their relationship had become. He couldn't bear to meet her eyes, pulling her into an embrace and murmuring in her hair, 'I'm sorry, Joan, I'm so sorry.'

The queue shifted forward and once more his eyes flicked to the window.

———

The remains of their supper were laid out in front of them, and he gazed at the mountain of chips, unable to comprehend how he ever managed to eat so much when he was younger.

The sound of the chair scraping against tarmac caught his attention. Joan was standing, her eyes fixated on the beach.

'Joan?'

Pushing the chair aside, she set off, striding towards the sea.

'Joan! Stop – wait a minute, please!' He hastily stuffed the remainder of the chips into a plastic bag, using the metal arms of the chair to lever himself to his feet. His body betrayed him regularly these days, and it took two attempts.

'Damn.'

She was moving away from him quicker than he thought possible, and he pushed his joints forward despite their best efforts to slow him down.

Gulls shrieked, circling above, greedily eyeing the leftovers bag.

Joan was on the beach now, her court shoes not made for sand, feet sinking heavily with every step, and he was grateful that his own misjudged choice offered him the opportunity to catch up.

Waves crashed onto the beach, and he knew if he licked his lips, he would taste their salt.

He stumbled to a halt next to her. She had removed her shoes, clutching them both in the hand furthest from him. Joan searched the horizon, her gaze sharper than he had seen it in months. He didn't want to break the spell, but he wanted to know what she was thinking. These moments were becoming less frequent. Tentatively, he brushed his fingers with hers, taking her hand. It was like paper, dry and light. She glanced down, then she passed him her shoes, bringing his hand to her lips for a kiss.

'You're still a funny looking chap, but you've grown on me over the years.'

His heart soared. He had found the treasure chest, and it was brimming with gold.

ANOTHER PARTING

CATH STAINCLIFFE

She sees him arrive, watches him step out of a blue Ford Cortina. She's looking through the kitchen window at the side of the club while the urn comes back to boil for the first of the teapots.

Her hands grip the edge of the sink, taking in all the ways he is familiar and all the ways he is strange.

Ten years.

He looks taller but his suit, slim and black, probably accounts for that.

His hair is even longer, below his shoulders, dark, glossy. The woman with him is dark haired, too, and almost his height. Have they travelled up today? Where was it, Coventry or Wolverhampton? Somewhere down there.

She takes the teapot and hot water through to the clubroom and sets them beside the buffet. The platters of sandwiches, sausage rolls, stand pie and quiche Lorraine are covered with white linen cloths. Cups and saucers in muddy green utility crockery at the ready.

She can hear voices from the hall. People shedding coats, visiting the toilets. The first of the funeral party.

'All set?' Her mum is behind the bar.

'Yes. I'll hop on now?'

Her mum nods.

He doesn't come to buy drinks himself. She concentrates on pulling pints and opening bottles of Pony and Babycham. Greeting members of his family, neighbours and friends. Listening to the chatter about the service, about the location of the plot at the graveyard and the weather, the rain holding off. And how it's a blessing really when she had been so poorly.

He is sitting at one of the tables at the far side, opposite the bar, where the large windows give views onto the moors.

The edge of nowhere, she thinks. The day is dull, the sky overcast, with clouds like boulders. The hills a hundred shades of brown. Dun coloured grass and spikes of rusting dock. Here and there a spill of moss, vivid green.

That summer they spent hours up here, hot and giddy. Time snatched from holiday jobs and chores. The prick of grass on her shoulder blades, his hair falling in curtains as he kissed her. The air thick with insects. The rushing of the beck and the burble of songbirds.

He looks across now, straight at her. Tips his head, with a ghost of a smile. Her mouth dries.

She wipes her hands on a bar towel and says to her mum, 'Shall I do the buffet?'

There's a pause, the slightest pause, then her mum says, 'Yes, if you like.'

She brings out the trifle and the gateau from the fridge. She is watching herself perform. Aware of the set of her shoulders, the belt at her waist, the curve of her arm as she plucks cloths from the trays of savouries, piling the fabric over one arm.

Keeping her chin level she walks to his table.

He stands to meet her.

'Tina.' He smiles, tremulous.

'Jed. I'm sorry about your nan.' The woman who raised him.

'Thanks.'

She is aware of the table taking in their encounter. His cousins, his wife. Does she know? Has he told her?

'The buffet is ready. I'll just bring fresh tea.'

'Thank you.' His fist, at his side, is clenched tight, knuckles white.

As she moves away he taps his beer glass with a teaspoon to quieten the room and announces that they are to please help themselves.

She fetches the tea and more water for coffee.

Max Bygraves is replaced by Dusty Springfield, the volume low so people can hear themselves think.

She can smell her own body odour in spite of the roll-on she used first thing.

In the ladies, she wets paper towels, adds a daub of soap. She strips off in the cubicle to wash her armpits.

He is still beautiful.

People are laughing, sharing anecdotes, the volume level rising as they relax, as the food and drinks go down.

She takes a turn on the bar while her mum has a break. Then they swap.

Outside, she sits on one of the cast iron benches and smokes. Watches the rooks, beaks stabbing at the ground. She feels a fine spot of rain on her cheek, then another.

She twists round at the sound of footsteps.

'Hello,' Jed says. 'Great buffet.'

'Thanks.'

'Who should I pay? I've a cheque.'

'My mum... or I can take it.'

He rummages in his inside jacket pocket, pulls it out.

She takes it, folded.

'You're not going to read it?'

'I trust you.' She laughs. Then feels stupid. Why? She does trust him. Always did.

'Got a spare cig?'

'Sure.' She hands him the packet

He sits, uses her lighter to spark up.

'You're married,' she says.

'Four years.'

'She looks nice.'

'Yeah.' He clears his throat. Then he turns to her. 'She's expecting,' he says. A flash in his eyes. Fear. At the fact of it? Or at how she'll react?

'Right,' she says. 'Congratulations.'

'You've not...?'

'Not yet. We'd like to, obviously.'

'Back then...' he says. His eyes fill with tears. Her nose waters in response.

'I know,' she says quickly. 'We were too young.'

'Maybe,' he says, a break in his voice.

'We were,' she says. 'Kids ourselves.'

She takes a final drag of her cigarette, crushes the tab end underfoot.

'I would have—'

'I know. But it was best all round.' She has to believe this or she would go mad. She wonders who the child favours, but briefly, fleetingly. It's not something to dwell on.

'I best get back,' she says.

'Look after yourself,' he says. He sniffs hard.

———

When they are done and the place cleared and cleaned, she takes the rubbish out to the bin.

Her mother locks up.

'You all right, Tina?' she says, buttoning up her coat. And her eyes settle on Tina's, searching.

'I'm fine, Mum,' she says. 'I'll be fine.'

NIPPLES, COILS AND COMPOST

ANDY STEWART

The ink wasn't running smoothly. Robina gave her fountain pen a shake and was rewarded by a messy blob of royal blue on the sleeve of her blouse. A biro would have been much more practical but she loved the flow of Quink onto the paper. She only used her stainless steel and gold Sonnet for signing prescriptions and death certificates. It was worth all the hassle of occasional blots as it added a flourish to an otherwise tedious task, and she loved the feel of the barrel between her fingers.

Mrs Haycroft entered the consulting room with her teenage son Gregory following morosely behind. He reminded Robina of a burdened donkey being led down a steep path on Santorini, an island she had enjoyed in the company of hedonistic Rory Riddleston three summers ago. She realised she was starting to entertain unsettling memories of sex in the Cyclades, and shook herself back to the here and now. Rory was long gone out of her life. Mrs Haycroft sat on one of two chairs on the other side of the consulting room desk while her son stood self-consciously behind the other.

"Do have a seat, Rory."

"His name's Gregory, Dr Jones."

"I'm so sorry, Mrs Haycroft. Confusing him with another patient. Do have a seat, Gregory." The youth dragged the chair backwards and settled on it so he was sitting directly behind his mother. "What can I do for you, Mrs Haycroft?"

"I'm worried that someone has been putting things in his drinks at school. Either that or he's been to one of these gender realignment clinics without telling us."

Robina studied Hilary Haycroft. Mrs H was in her early forties, wearing a green anorak done up to the neck and dark blue chinos. She had no makeup on. Her eyes darted from Robina to the wall behind and back again.

"What do you think someone's been putting in his drinks?"

"Hormones. He says he's growing breasts."

Robina heard a groan coming from behind Mrs Haycroft. Either that was Gregory suffering agonies of embarrassment or his mother was an accomplished ventriloquist.

"How old is Gregory?"

"Thirteen. And a bit."

"Hello, Gregory." Robina addressed her remarks into the air behind the boy's mother.

"Ullo."

"If you bring your chair round here, I can get a better look at you," said Robina using her kind and caring voice.

With a lot of shuffling and grunting the ungainly lad reappeared beside his mother. He achieved this whilst remaining seated and scraping the chair along the ground. He wore a grey school blazer and a chaotically knotted grey and yellow tie. His face was decorated with scattered acne clusters.

"I'm sure this is nothing to worry about. Why don't you get onto the examination couch over there and take your jacket, tie and shirt off? You can draw the curtains round so you have some privacy. Let me know when you're ready."

After what seemed to Robina like enough time for him to have had a bath and read a short novel, Gregory's breaking voice warbled. "Ready."

Robina parted the curtains and smiled to ease his anxiety. She closed the drapes behind her. He blushed deeply. She rubbed her hands together to warm them and hoped he didn't misinterpret this considerate act as her rubbing her hands with glee. He winced as she examined around both his nipples, screwing his eyelids tightly together to avoid seeing what was going on.

"You have a tiny lump behind both nipples. Fifty percent of boys get these little swellings during puberty. It's due to changes in the levels of hormones in your body; all part of growing up. It's perfectly normal and nothing to worry about. The little bumps will be gone in a few months."

"So, I'm not growing boobs?"

"Definitely not."

He opened his eyes. "And I won't have to wear a bra?"

Robina shook her head.

"Should he have a mammogram, doctor? Just to make sure it's nothing serious."

Doctor and patient turned as one to see Mrs Haycroft poking her head through the curtains. Gregory placed his hands over his nipples.

"Absolutely not needed, but I am happy to check Gregory's chest again in a few months' time just to reassure you both."

"As long as you're sure, doctor. How long have you been qualified?"

"I'm older than I look, Mrs Haycroft. Gregory, would you like something to help with those spots. What are you using at the moment?"

Before the teenager could answer his mother spoke. "Clearasil. He gets through so many bottles I think he must be drinking it."

"Slip your things back on, Gregory, and come and have a seat. I'll give you a booklet to read about acne and I'll prescribe some antibiotics to kill the bacteria that are making the spots worse, plus a cream to rub in at night so your skin is less oily."

After Gregory and his mother had left the room, Bathsheba brought a coffee in for Robina.

"Milk with no sugar," the receptionist said, plonking the mug down so hard on the desk that some of its contents splashed out.

"Thanks. You're very kind."

"We like to look after our locum doctors, just to make sure they come back again. That's a beautiful pen. I've never seen one like it. Was it a present?"

"Yes. From me to me. And as we're exchanging compliments, Bathsheba, that's a lovely dress you're wearing. The colours are stunning. It really suits your skin tone."

The receptionist beamed. "Most surgeries make you wear a uniform, but Dr Greenskin says he doesn't care how we're dressed as long as we don't turn up in just our undies. I'll tell your next patient to come in. It's Mr Priggis. He usually comes to discuss his wife."

Robina wasn't sure how Bathsheba knew what Mr Priggis was going to talk about as consultations were supposed to be confidential, but decided it was better not to ask if she wanted to keep getting brought mugs of coffee.

Alan Priggis walked in. He looked in his mid-forties with a paunch peeking over his belt. He pulled up a chair and, leaning both elbows on the desk, looked steadily into Robina's eyes. "I'm here to talk about my wife." He had a blue and white hooped too-tight rugby shirt on, with his thinning locks carefully brushed over a receding hairline.

"Does Mrs Priggis know you're here?"

"She thinks I'm at the garden centre buying peat-free compost."

"Peat-free?"

"It's better for the planet. Peat bogs store carbon, oodles of it. The equivalent of twenty years of industrial carbon is stored in British peat bogs. If you dig them up, all that carbon gets released into the atmosphere. Ecological disaster."

"About your wife…"

"Also, peat bogs are home to a huge number of flora and fauna including snipes, butterflies and dragonflies."

"You were here to talk about your wife?"

"What? Oh, yes, I'm worried about her. I think she may be depressed."

"What makes you think that?"

"She's gone off sex. Says she can't be bothered. Going on for months."

"Any other signs of depression?"

"Only if I mention moving myself out of the spare room back to our double bed."

"How are things otherwise between you?"

"Hunky-dory."

"Your wife might find it helpful to come in for a chat. Do you think she'd agree to see me? Unfortunately, it's not easy getting appointments at the moment."

"You're not bloody kidding. I waited a month for this one. I'll see what she says. Don't tell her I've been in to see you."

After Alan Priggis had departed, Bathsheba came bustling in to retrieve Robina's empty mug.

"Mrs Priggis is coming in to see you this afternoon."

"Bloody hell! That was quick."

"Not really. She made the appointment a month ago. Enjoy your lunch break. You've got ten minutes before afternoon surgery starts. You could nip to the garage on the corner. They sell what they claim are sandwiches."

Ten minutes later, Robina was back behind her consulting desk. She pressed the stiff intercom button that connected her to the seething waiting room, having to depress it forcibly several times before she heard the howling banshee screech that confirmed it was functioning. Waves of ferocious heartburn swept across her stomach as a result of rapid wolfing down of tuna and sweetcorn wedged between sheets of what tasted like soggy cardboard. Using her London Underground mind-the-gap voice she summoned Mrs Barbara Priggis to come and join her in consulting room number three. As the door swung open, a sonorous burp escaped Robina's lips.

"I'm so sorry, Mrs Priggis. I've eaten something that's disagreed with me."

"I know how you feel. My husband's always disagreeing with me."

Mrs Priggis had a no-nonsense air about her. Not a hair out of place and no hint of depressive illness. Her tailored aquamarine jacket and skirt accentuated her womanly shape whilst suggesting she shopped at John Lewis rather than M&S.

Robina hiccupped. Several times. "What can I do for you?"

"I'd like to have a coil fitted."

Following her conversation earlier with Alan Priggis, this statement took Robina by surprise. Then she thought about it. Of course, a fear of pregnancy could easily have an adverse effect on libido.

"Do you have any *(hiccup)* children, Mrs Priggis?"

"Two. Ten and eight."

"And how old are you now?"

"Thirty-six."

"Looking at your notes *(hiccup)* I see you used to take the oral contraceptive pill."

"Didn't suit me. Put on weight and got awful migraines, in spite of trying several different ones. Had a go with the cap after that but it was a devil trying to get it in the right position, and it kept jumping out of me like a rabbit from a magician's hat. So, then we used rubbers."

Robina decided she needed to proceed carefully. "Do you have *(hiccup hiccup)* intercourse regularly?"

"Depends what you mean by regularly. When I can, is the honest answer. How often do you have intercourse, Dr Jones?"

Robina tried not to look rattled. Not often enough at the moment; in fact, not at all this year. At least the shock of Mrs Priggis' repost had banished her hiccups. "I need to check it's safe to fit you with an intrauterine device. Have you ever had an ectopic pregnancy?"

"Not as far as I know."

"Or any pelvic infections?"

"Just the odd bit of thrush, but nothing more serious than that."

"I'm going to give you a leaflet to take home that will tell you all about the different types of coil. It should answer any questions you have. I'm family planning trained so I could fit it for you but we'd need to set aside time which we don't have today."

"Do you believe my body is mine to do with as I wish?"

"Absolutely."

The patient's brow furrowed. "This is all confidential, isn't it?"

"Of course. As are all consultations."

"Good. I don't want my husband to know about this." She wheeled round and departed clutching her leaflet.

"You don't want..." started Robina, her words falling on empty air as the proverbial penny dropped with a virtual clatter. Mrs Priggis was having an affair. If her husband consulted Robina again about his wife's loss of libido what on earth could she say to the man? Perhaps she could steer their conversation towards peat-free compost.

Bathsheba came in with yet another mug of coffee. "That Barbara Priggis, she's having it off with Ben Nicholls at the post office. I expect that why she wants you to fit her with a coil."

"Are you a mind reader, Bathsheba?"

"No. You left the intercom switched on. I forgot to warn you about that button. Everyone in the waiting room was listening and, until you turn it off, they still are."

NOT NORMAL

JUDY WALKER

So, here they were. In Greece. For a holiday, a break, a chance to put things into perspective, a fresh start. Whatever you wanted to call it after your husband has had an affair.

He wheeled the cases in from the car. She walked through the living room towards the patio doors, opened them and stepped out. A lovely spot. A glorious view. She sighed and turned back inside. In the kitchen there was a welcome pack on the table – wine, coffee, fruit, baklava. A nice touch.

"I'll take these upstairs, shall I?" He indicated the cases.

"Yeah. I'll come up with you."

Two bedrooms. He hovered between them.

"So… do you want…?"

"For God's sake, Ian. We'll sleep in the same room. That's what this is all about, isn't it?" Her tone was sharp. She often allowed it to be so, now. Just as she allowed her anger to erupt. So much anger. She had never been an angry person, so where did it all come from? When they argued – something else they never used to do – she shouted and screamed, threw things, told him she hated him. She'd never done that before, but then he'd never done what he did before.

He was such a different person now. He'd shown her a completely new side to himself – the man who lived high in La La Land, enjoying his exciting new relationship, not giving a moment's thought to her feelings but still insisting that he loved her, telling her she had nothing to worry about, that it was over. Except, of course, it wasn't really.

They unpacked and settled in. They took a walk to the shop and bought food and more wine. Back at the house she began preparing dinner – just cold stuff with olives and bread.

"Would you like a drink?" He held up the bottle of wine. His tone courteous, polite.

"Yes, thank you. That would be nice," she replied, also polite, a little formal.

This was not the way a long-time married couple spoke to each other, was it? This was not normal.

Not at all normal. She thought about that a lot. It was what she had told him when it was clear that the 'relationship' was continuing, because he could see nothing wrong in that – it was now merely platonic. He had conceded it was "unusual".

He brushed against her. "Sorry."

"It's ok." She said it automatically, but actually, she thought, it wasn't ok. She didn't want him touching her, not now, not anymore. That was the lasting damage.

Today was their wedding anniversary – their thirty-first. Nothing special to celebrate. Certainly, no cards had been exchanged. No mention of it had been made; unlike last year, their thirtieth anniversary. They'd celebrated with a party. She remembered feeling proud of the landmark, considered it quite an achievement to stay married to the same person for thirty years.

"More wine?" He tilted the bottle towards her glass.

"No thanks."

His drinking had increased. Not to a worrying level, but definitely too much. If they opened a bottle of wine, she would have a couple of glasses, while he saw off the rest. Then he'd open another bottle or pour himself a whisky, often two. He'd bought a bottle of Metaxa at the duty-free.

———

They sat, watching the sun go down, making conversation as needed. She went to bed before him.

In the morning, she woke early, as always, silently picked up her phone, opened his company website and clicked on the 'our team' page to stare at the two pictures of her, as she had done every morning, since that day in November when he'd told her. She looked at the brown eyes and the long fair hair, many strands of which she had picked off his clothes in the last few months. She closed the website and cleared her history.

They fell into a routine. She would walk to the shop to get stuff for breakfast, which they ate on the terrace. She read her book while he looked at the paper on his phone. That's what he said he was doing, anyway. Some days they took a stroll into the village for coffee or lunch. In the afternoons, he went for a swim while she stayed at the villa or went for long walks, still trying to get everything straight in her head. In the evenings, they went out to eat, or sometimes she would make a meal. It was all very pleasant, very amicable, civilised. She kept an eye on the mark on his back.

That day in November. She'd come in from work. He was already home.

"Come and sit down for a minute," he'd said. "I want to talk to you about something."

Her first thought was that it was a health issue, another melanoma. When he told her he'd been having a 'thing' – was that how he'd described it? She couldn't remember now, but she knew he hadn't called it an affair or a relationship – she was shocked, but not surprised because, she realised, she already knew. He talked about her all the time – a classic tell. He spent a lot of time on his phone in the evenings when they were watching tv.

It had happened gradually. They worked on a couple of projects together, got on well, shared a sense of humour. He was very anxious – too anxious – to assure her that they hadn't slept together. She knew that was a lie, one of the many that had followed over the previous six months. The last time they had made love – had sex would be a more accurate description – he couldn't wait to pull away from her. That's how she knew he'd slept with her, Theresa, her name was. She was, of course, twenty years younger than him.

But, he said, he realised it was getting out of hand and so he had ended it. Except he hadn't really because he wanted to have his cake and eat it. He called it a pre-affair and said he had stopped it before it went too far, whatever that meant.

Now they were just back to being friends, colleagues. It was platonic. He kept using that word.

The texting continued, increased. Some days she counted thirty texts that he had sent her and she had responded with just as many. He thought he was being discreet but she would catch him with his phone while he was putting the bin out, getting something from the car, pretending it was a work message. His phone went with him everywhere, even the toilet. She had challenged him on this. "It's convenient to text in the toilet," he'd said. She had tried to picture the logistics of this, for a man.

She saw he'd sent texts to her at midnight after they had gone to bed. Who was this man who could lie and deceive with such ease?

This was before he'd become tech savvy, before he'd learned how to delete messages and turn off the sound notification, before he changed his passcode.

Again and again, they argued. Again and again, he said he would end it. But somehow it never happened. There was always a reason – excuse – for him to continue – she was ill, overwhelmed by work, lonely.

Until finally, one day, she snapped. Things had been going ok. She'd tried to ignore it, told herself she was being unreasonable – it was just a few texts. They had gone out for her birthday and had a nice meal at her favourite restaurant. He went to the toilet just before they left. When they got home, she looked at his phone and saw he'd sent her a text with a photo of the wine they'd had – from the timing, it was while he was in the toilet. She screamed at him, slammed doors, slept in the spare room. Next morning, she packed a bag and drove off. He rang her phone again and again. She ignored it.

She must have driven for a couple of hours, not really taking any notice of where she was going. Eventually, she pulled in at a brown sign for a picnic spot and country park, got out and started walking. In her mind she tried to play out every scenario – stay, leave, insist he left the company, let it carry on, confront her. Her head felt it might explode.

She thought of the time she had gone to the pub to pick him up after a work night out. She remembered greeting colleagues she'd met previously and being introduced to new ones. Now she wondered what they had been thinking when they saw her: *do you think she knows?* She imagined their pity for her. Her stomach curdled and sour bile rose in her throat. She swallowed it back down again.

If she left, what would she do? They'd been together so long. She didn't want to upset their boys. She tried to imagine how awkward it would be if one of their sons got married. How awkward it would be at any family celebration or get-together. It would spoil everything. Then there was the thought of moving to some miserable little house or flat, which made her shudder. Yet, in magazines, she had read about women just like her who had started afresh, met another man. Everything was wonderful. Could she take that risk? Perhaps she was just not being objective enough. She hadn't confided in anyone about Ian's behaviour. Maybe if she had, a friend might have told her she was being too sensitive about it. It was just texts.

Eventually, she turned back. When she got home, he just stood there, ashen-faced, his arms hanging limply at his sides. "Sorry, I'm sorry," he said. "I've ended it now."

She looked at him. "Why would I believe that?" she said.

"Why would I ever believe anything you ever say to me again, after all the lies you've told me?"

"I know. I'm sorry. I don't expect you to… but all I can say is that it really is finished this time."

She went upstairs, unpacked in the spare room. She couldn't bear to sleep in the same bed as him.

Later, when she was in the kitchen, he came in.

"I've been a good husband, haven't I? In thirty years, this is the first, the only… it's such a small thing. It's… it's nothing. It means nothing."

Over the following days they returned to some sort of normality. They had to because it was exhausting.

Then he suggested the holiday and she agreed.

They had been there a few days and things were going reasonably well, she thought. She went into the bedroom to get a beach wrap. His phone was on the bed so, from habit, she picked it up. There was a message showing on the lock screen. It was from her. Her hands shook as she opened it. There was a long thread, going back a week or so. It was just stuff about work, in-jokes. But they were cosy, intimate even. It was defi-nitely more than a friendship. It was still a relationship. It wasn't ever going to go away. As Princess Diana had famously once said, there were three people in their marriage. It was, she knew, up to her to decide whether that made it too crowded.

On their last night there they ate at the villa. She set the food on the table and sat down opposite him, pushed a stray hair behind her ear, released a breath from between her lips. She looked straight at him. His eyes were focused on her face, terrified, like the accused awaiting the jury's verdict.

"So… I think… I've thought long and hard about it and I think because, you know, on balance… that we… I should…" She looked out at the sea, blue and shimmering, then turned her eyes back to him, "risk it."

KIDNAPPED

GERALD WEBBER

The lady with the crayons was here again yesterday. Her name is Mrs Pearson but she tells me I should call her Tracey. Whatever. I don't like her. She smells of plasticine and old biscuits and she wears a hat that looks like a tea cosy. I expect her head is cold because her hair is short and spiky, like a man's, except that she dyes it pink, probably to make sure that people know she's a woman. I don't really know why she comes, but she says she's "just looking out" for me, whatever that means.

"Let's draw a picture of your house, shall we?" she says. She sounds like she used to be a teacher, pretending to be happy and interested in what I'm doing. But that's not how she looks to me. Her eyes are sad and she wears little round glasses with metal frames, like the baddies do on telly. I don't think she likes children. That's probably why they stopped her from being a teacher. Plus her crayons are broken, and she keeps them all together in an old tin that has a picture on the lid of a soldier in a black hat and a lady in a bonnet. Real teachers store them in cardboard packets and write "2b" on the back with a felt-tip pen.

So I draw our house with four windows and a front door in the middle, like I know you should, even though we live in a flat, and Mrs Pearson looks at it and says, "That's nice. Now let's draw the people who live in the house, shall we?", as if she was playing with the crayons as well. If she had been, I reckon she'd have drawn a big black house with a cat outside. Then she sits next to me on the sofa, which I don't much like, and I notice that the skin on her hands is all thin and wrinkly, which I don't like either.

I draw mum in a blue dress with yellow hair and red lips, and dad with a big brown beard. He's larger than she is, of course, and nearly as tall as the house, although actually he's not that big. But we don't live in a house anyway, so it doesn't really matter. Then I draw myself in between them. My head is round and I add a smiley face, which is what you do. Then I colour it pink, a bit like Mrs Pearson's hair. "Are mummy and daddy happy too?", she asks, stupidly. Of course they aren't, because dad has disappeared, which she knows already. So I ignore her and add some clouds and rain above the house instead. I don't like Mrs Pearson.

"Are you just here until my dad gets back?", I ask her.

"Something like that", she says. "Your mother is very unhappy at the moment and she's worried about your father because he hasn't been at all nice to her, and we don't know where he is right now, so I'm just here to help make sure that you're alright, until we get everything sorted out. Ok?" I don't know what she and the man in the grey suit have done with my dad, but I'm starting to think that he might have escaped, which is why they don't know where he is any more. I hope so anyway, because I miss him.

"Ok", I say.

———

The man in the grey suit is always writing things down in his notebook, as if he can't remember what anyone says, which isn't normal. I think he's probably sending messages to other members of the gang. So I'm careful what I say. He says he is a policeman, but obviously he isn't because he doesn't wear a uniform, and he doesn't drive a police car. He tells me that he's Inspector something-or-other, but that I can call him Mr Sherman. Or David. But I don't call him anything.

His handwriting slopes the wrong way and his letters are small and wavy, so I think he might be writing in code, which is what they do. He has hairs growing out of his nose, so I can't bear to look at him for long, even though he tells me to, and when I do I try to focus on his eyebrows, which are dark and bushy, as if he's stuck them on, which he might have done, I suppose. They use disguises when they can't wear masks.

"So, when was the last time you saw your father?", he says. We were sitting at the kitchen table. Mrs Pearson was there as well. Mr Sherman had a silver pen in his hand and was leaning on our second-best tablecloth with his sleeves rolled up, so the plastic kept sticking to his arms. The room smelled of cooking fat and aftershave. "The day before he disappeared", I said. "On Monday". I remembered because we always have maca-roni cheese out of a tin on Mondays, which I like. Mum says we have to because it's all she can afford, but I don't care about that.

"And how was your mother when you went to bed that evening?", he asks. "Same as normal", I say, shrugging my shoulders. I thought that was clever, because it was true. She's always crying and shaky, which is why she has those tablets from the doctors. "Did you see or hear anything unusual that night?", he asked. I looked at his eyebrows. "No", I said, and then I shut up. I didn't want to get anyone into trouble. But I wasn't sure if that was the right answer, so I turned to Mrs Pearson and asked if I could go back to the other room and do some more drawing instead. They let me go, and I opened the tin of crayons to find a red one, which I scribbled with until I'd covered the whole of the paper, and my arm was tired.

————

My granny is looking after me while mum is in the hospital. She's here most of the time at the moment and stays overnight, when Mrs Pearson and the man in the suit aren't around. But I'm not sure I can trust her to keep a secret, so I don't say much about mum and dad, just in case. I don't see granny very often as a rule, and I don't think she likes talking to me really. In any case, I don't know what we'd talk about. She spends most of the time watching telly or doing stuff on her phone, and I know she doesn't like my dad, so I think that she might be helping the others.

She's nothing like my mum. Granny has a skinny face and brown hair that she pulls back in a pony-tail. I suppose she thinks it makes her look young, but it doesn't, because she isn't. She's not as fat as some of the grannies I've seen on our estate, but she shouldn't wear tee-shirts and trackie-bottoms, and she shouldn't smoke or swear so much, or drink lager out of a can either. Real grannies aren't like that. To be fair, she doesn't drink when Mrs Pearson is around though, which is kind of her because I know that Mrs Pearson isn't happy about the empty cans and the smell of granny's home-made cigarettes. But I don't like Mrs Pearson more than I don't like granny, so I pretend not to notice.

——————

My friend Darren sent me a message on the PS4 the other day. We were playing *Assassin's Creed*, the new one, which my dad bought me for Christmas. According to Darren's mum the mothers on our estate think my dad's a "fucking animal", but Darren tells me that his mum says things like that about lots of people so I shouldn't worry about it. I tell Darren that I think my dad's been kidnapped and that he'd better be careful what he says to his mum because it sounds like she might be part of the gang as well. I tell him about Mrs Pearson and Mr Sherman and about my granny, who hates my dad and is always sending secret messages to people on her phone, and I tell him that I think my dad might now be on the run after escaping from the bad guys, which is why they're keeping me in the flat and my mum in a hospital, so they can catch him when he comes back to rescue us. I tell Darren that he could be in danger too, if anyone finds out we've been talking. Then I stab a foot-soldier in the neck, which completes the mission. Darren promises not to say anything to his mum.

It was almost ten o'clock when Mrs Pearson woke me up. Granny had let me sleep in and gone to the shops for some cigarettes, apparently.

"Your mum's here", she said. "So get yourself dressed and we'll go through to the other room and see her. But remember that she's had a difficult time and she's a bit woozy with all the drugs. She's got some bruises and some stitches on her face, and her arm's in a sling, so don't be frightened by any of that when you see her. Ok? The doctors have taken good care of her and she's on the mend now, so she'll be fine. Come on. Let's go through, shall we?"

Mum looked worse than I expected. Her lips were swollen, and the side of her face was bruised. The skin around her left eye was dark and shiny, but it was difficult to know what colour it was because there aren't any crayons like that. Her hair was messy, as if she'd just got out of bed, and there were four black stitches on her cheek.

"Come here, darling", she said, and leaned forward to hug me with her free hand. She smelled of sticking plasters and old pyjamas. "Tracey tells me you've been a good boy while I've been away, and that you haven't cried once. That's brave" she said and kissed me on the top of the head before letting me go. I didn't know what to say, so I didn't say anything. She wiped her eyes with a paper handkerchief, then blew her nose with it.

"Now, I think you know from Tracey and the inspector that daddy and I had a bit of a fight the other night. Yes?" I nodded, half-remembering the noises that had woken me up. I had peeked through the crack in the bedroom door to see mum shouting and crying and wiping lipstick across her face with the back of her hand. I had run back to bed and hidden under the sheets, pretending to be asleep until the morning because I didn't like it when she was drunk. "Well, now that they've let me out of hospital, Tracey has found us somewhere new to live. Somewhere safe. So I want you to get dressed and pack some clothes in the suitcase that you take on holiday so that we can go. Now. Alright? Don't worry if you forget anything. Granny can bring it later."

I was about to tell her that I didn't want to go when I realised that she was frightened, and that she had to do what Mrs Pearson said, or the gang would beat her up again.

"Ok", I said.

ABOUT THE HENSHAW PRESS SHORT STORY COMPETITION

Henshaw Press is a small imprint that runs the four-times-a-year not-for-profit Henshaw Press Short Story Competition.

Henshaw Press was launched by a small group of writers, editors, lecturers and of course readers who wished to actively support creative writing. They ran quarterly competitions throughout the year with closing dates at the end of March, June, September and December.

The competition is still going strong, albeit under new management (Hobeck Books). The competition asks for original stories of up to 2,000 words on any subject, and is open to anyone over the age of sixteen. The fee for entry is just £6. For each competition there is a first prize award of £200, second prize of £100 and third prize of £50. The competition is open to anyone, anywhere, from any background.

If you are under sixteen, all is not lost, you can send your short story to Henshaw Press to get a free critique by an expert in the field.

Henshaw Press also offers critiques to competition entrants, for a fee of £14.

If you are interested in entering, please check the website www.henshawpress.co.uk for details.

All profits from the competitions and the publishing of the anthologies go towards buying books for schools.

In 2023, the Christopher Whitehead Language College and Sixth Form in Worcester received a donation of £406.39.

For 2024, Burton Borough High School in Newport, Shropshire, received a donation of £581.40.

The recipient of profits for 2025 and from the sale of this anthology will be Walton High School in Stafford.

The more entries we get, the more sales we get, the more money we can raise!

HOBECK BOOKS – THE HOME OF GREAT STORIES

We hope you've enjoyed reading this anthology, which is published by Hobeck Books.

We offer a number of our authors' own short stories and novellas, free for subscribers in the compilation *Crime Bites*. Simply subscribe to www.hobeck.net to claim your free copy. As a subscriber, you will also receive our weekly newsletter plus updates on all our publishing news and competitions.

- *Echo Rock* by Robert Daws
- *Old Dogs, Old Tricks* by AB Morgan
- *The Silence of the Rabbit* by Wendy Turbin
- *Never Mind the Baubles: An Anthology of Twisted Winter Tales* by the Hobeck Team (including many of the Hobeck authors and Hobeck's two publishers)
- *The Clarice Cliff Vase* by Linda Huber
- *Here She Lies* by Kerena Swan
- *Fatal Beginnings* by Brian Price
- *A Defining Moment* by Lin Le Versha

- *Saviour* by Jennie Ensor
- *You Can't Trust Anyone These Days* by Maureen Myant

Please visit the Hobeck Books website for details of our other superb authors and their books, and if you would like to get in touch, we would love to hear from you.

Hobeck Books also presents a weekly podcast, the Hobcast, where founders Adrian Hobart and Rebecca Collins discuss all things book related, key issues from each week, including the ups and downs of running a creative business. Each episode includes an interview with one of the people who make Hobeck possible: the editors, the authors, the cover designers. These are the people who help Hobeck bring great stories to life. Without them, Hobeck wouldn't exist. The Hobcast can be listened to from all the usual platforms but it can also be found on the Hobeck website: **www.hobeck.net/hobcast**.

If you like short stories, Hobeck Books has also published two Christmas charity anthologies: *The Dark Side of Christmas* and *Cooking the Books*.

www.ingramcontent.com/pod-product-compliance
Lightning Source LLC
Chambersburg PA
CBHW010436170726
48283CB00011B/3231